*A
Harlequin
Romance*

OTHER
Harlequin Romances
by MARGARET PARGETER

THE KILTED STRANGER

by

MARGARET PARGETER

Harlequin Books

TORONTO • LONDON • NEW YORK • AMSTERDAM • SYDNEY • WINNIPEG

Original hardcover edition published in 1975
by Mills & Boon Limited

SBN 373-01973-4

Harlequin edition published May, 1976

CHAPTER ONE

IT was August and the midday sun was hot. Susan Granger's smoky grey eyes followed the dancing rays of it across the white-tabled restaurant. When another diner complained she noticed that the young proprietor walked over to the window and drew the thin cotton curtains, effectively cutting out the glare. The curtains were made of a brown cotton material with a white geometric pattern on it. They were attractive. Sue hadn't noticed them before. They looked new. Carefully, her attention caught, she forgot the man she was having lunch with and stared.

'Susan!' Tim Mason's impatient exclamation made no impact even when it sharpened on the last syllables of her name. It wasn't until he spoke again that her wandering gaze returned to fix itself unhappily on his face.

'I'm sorry,' she murmured, shrivelling a little beneath his withering regard, grateful when the waitress arrived with their coffee, creating a diversion. It had been a mistake to come here with Tim today, but he had been so insistent. He couldn't be expected to understand that she still found it difficult to concentrate. Along with other things the shock of her mother's accident had done this to her. That man with the curtains . . . Was it strange that such a simple everyday performance should bring such a comforting sense of normality? A reassurance which all Tim's effusive sympathy and stringent advice had failed to give.

'I'm sorry,' she repeated, as he stirred his coffee angrily, lasping into a rather sullen silence as the waitress went.

His sandy brows raised and he shot her a quick look, not bothering to hide a faint hint of reproach. 'I wouldn't mind, darling, but my lunch hour doesn't go on indefinitely, and old Wilcox will have a fit if I'm so much as five minutes late. You might at least listen to what I'm saying. I was asking you about that letter. Now that you've had time to think things over, you aren't still considering it seriously, are you?'

Looking away from him quickly, Sue gazed uncertainly down at her hands. 'And what if I am?' she asked defiantly.

'Oh, Sue!' His eyes probed her pale face despairingly. 'To begin with – well, that wasn't hard to understand, but surely it's time you began to think rationally?'

Resentment flared, bringing a surge of colour to her pale cheeks, a healthier sparkle to her sombre eyes. 'I did promise.' She swallowed painfully. 'The last promise that I'll ever make.'

Tim's good-looking face darkened and he gave a small grunt. 'I think you're being far too dramatic, Sue,' he said. He leant nearer, across the table, suddenly intent. 'You can tell me to mind my own business if you like, but you've devoted all your life to your mother – she saw to it that you never had much real freedom.' As Sue started to protest he threw up a restraining hand. 'She asked you to deliver this letter when she was really too ill to have known what she was asking. Don't you see, Sue, it could mean more strings, and I think you've had quite enough of those. You've never even heard of the person to whom this letter is addressed. It could be some old relative – almost sure to be if she wrote it some time ago. Whoever it is they'll probably be in need of care and attention, and knowing you, you'll be unable to refuse!'

Sue's hands clenched nervously beneath the table. Tim had no right to speak to her like this. She didn't belong to him in any way, nor did she want to. Yet probably he only spoke as he did because he was anxious? 'Tim,' she faltered, 'you could be wrong. And I've told you before, Mother only wrote the letter a few weeks ago. She wasn't a very sensitive person, but she did get these sudden premonitions.' She

6

didn't allude to his other remarks, unable to deny the truth of them.

He wasn't impressed. She hadn't really expected he would be. He retorted dryly, his brown eyes sceptical, 'We can all imagine that we're going to have an accident, Sue. It's a sort of psychological impact. They happen every day. It must be my turn next – that sort of thing. Your mother was too highly strung to apply a little common sense.'

'It's not that exactly, Tim.' His voice cut cruelly across her ragged nerves. His air of disparagement set her teeth on edge. She wanted to get up and walk out, only some stubborn streak in her make-up kept her sitting where she was. 'You must see,' she went on, 'that this is something I feel I have to do whether I really want to or not. I don't particularly wish to go chasing off into the wilds of Scotland at the moment, but I did promise!'

'When you were naturally upset! If you'd just consider carefully, darling. Promises . . .' For the first time he hesitated, uncertain, not really intending to wound.

'Deathbed promises, you mean,' she prompted expressionlessly as he paused.

He muttered angrily, sensing her contempt, his eyes suddenly as hostile as hers. 'I suppose I do, but I wasn't going to put it so bluntly. Not many people are able to refuse requests at a time like that . . .' Carefully he spooned more sugar into his coffee, giving himself time to think.

'Look, Sue,' decisively he replaced his spoon in his saucer, 'can I be frank?'

Numbly, although slightly warily, she nodded, and he continued, his eyes gentler now on her smooth, beautifully boned face. 'I know you feel that this letter is very important, but so far as you're concerned I didn't trust your mother when she was alive, and I'm afraid I still don't now.'

'Please . . .'

But he didn't allow her small, protesting gasp to deter him. 'Just hear me out, Sue. It's only for your sake I'm saying

7

this. Sometimes I didn't think your mother liked you very much, which seemed strange, considering you were all she had. I've seen her gazing at you with the most peculiar expression in her eyes, almost as if she didn't care for what she saw. As if you reminded her of someone she didn't like, and no one could say you looked a bit like her. But – well, most of the time she was possessive, sometimes scarcely willing to let you out of her sight. Look at how she insisted you found a job in the immediate vicinity after you left college! She always wanted you near, but that doesn't prove how much she loved you. Of course it might just have been that she wasn't very maternal, but can you wonder if I'm suspicious about all this other business now?'

Sue flinched, her lips suddenly dry, her face paler as the logic of his words hurt, the pain spreading insidiously. She hadn't realized he'd been aware of so much. That his interest had been self-motivated she had little doubt. He wouldn't know how much it hurt to have one's private doubts and fears exposed to such cruel analysis. The relationship she had shared with her mother was something she never wanted to talk about, certainly not with Tim, with his methodical, detached way of looking at everything. 'I'd rather not discuss it,' she answered at last – very coolly.

Impatience flared again as he watched her dark-lashed eyes widen defensively. 'Sometimes I think I don't understand you at all, Sue,' he muttered, eyebrows and temper shooting up simultaneously.

Most of the time I don't understand you either, Sue felt like retorting. But she didn't; not aloud. After all, he had been kind and helped her a lot during these last few days, and appeared to be the only close friend she had. He had also been the only man in their small circle of acquaintances whom her mother had tolerated reasonably well. She looked at him, her grey eyes solemn. 'It hasn't been long, Tim, you could try to be tolerant.'

'I'm trying, Sue.' Across the table his deep sigh was quite audible. Then suddenly he was softly pleading, changing his tactics, bewildering her as he often did by his complete volte-face. 'Darling,' his hand crept across the table to cover her clenched one, 'why don't we get married? Then I could take care of everything. Your mother would have approved, I'm sure of that. Then I could be responsible for all your affairs, and if you insist we could deliver that mysterious letter together – maybe during my next holiday or long weekend.'

'Oh, Tim!' Tears came, and she wished she wasn't quite so jumpy. A hint of kindness still did this to her. Tears! Staring at him aghast, she blinked them back before he could notice. She hadn't reached the age of twenty without having gone through a handful of boy-friends. She was young and healthy and enjoyed her fun. Only most of them hadn't been a lot of fun really, not with her mother doing her best to antagonize them, and it had never seemed possible to keep them completely out of her way. Always there had been some fault, subtly yet sharply pointed out, effectively spoiling a gay but easily destructible relationship.

Looking back, Sue wondered why she had often given in so quickly. She sometimes fretted that she had reached the age she had without ever being in love. Was she too much like her mother, without any real capacity for deeper feelings? Or perhaps the emotions she dreamt about were totally unrealistic, the heady, warm, bubbling feelings a myth. She was extremely fond of Tim most of the time. Perhaps this was sufficient? But even as the thought entered her head she dismissed it. She knew that she couldn't agree to marry him, not yet. Not until she was completely sure.

'I'm sorry, Tim,' her voice trembled slightly as she attempted to hide her uncertainty, 'I just couldn't think of marrying anyone at the moment.'

Tim, looking into her pale, faintly flushed face, thought he understood. It was too soon after her bereavement. He had been too hasty. His hand tightened reassuringly over hers. 'Don't worry, darling, I'll ask you again. Just keep it in mind. But,' he frowned, glancing anxiously at his watch, 'you must promise me that you'll do nothing about this other matter without letting me know.'

Irrelevantly Sue wished he wouldn't keep calling her darling. It might give people the wrong impression. She felt something like a surge of relief when he didn't pursue the subject of marriage any further, but she didn't particularly want to promise him anything, not even brief details of her movements. It might be good to get away for a little while, but she wouldn't say so. There seemed little sense in hurting him deliberately and he might not understand.

Uncertainly she shrugged, glancing at him swiftly, curiously evasive. 'I'm not sure what I'll be doing, Tim,' she replied, gathering up her bag as he drained his coffee cup and signalled to the waitress, his lunch hour nearly over. 'Not until I've seen Mother's solicitor. I have an appointment with him this afternoon.'

A dry, late summer wind blew skittishly along the street as she parted from Tim outside the café and made her way towards the bus stop. It was too fine a day to take the tube, but the wind was disagreeable, whirling untidy bits of litter, stirring fine dust about her feet. Sue, taking a grip of herself, resisted a half-formed impulse to scruff her toes in it as the bored-looking schoolboy in front of her was doing. Instead she straightened her shoulders and told herself resolutely that London, even in August, could be nice. And if she didn't care for life in a huge city, there were thousands who did. Her mother had loved it, finding in the busy streets the anonymity she had always appeared to crave.

Sue sighed uneasily, hopping on to the bus when it came, seating herself precariously on the top deck, staring out through the window at the rows of houses and shops which obtruded on to her vision, then dissolved into a meaningless blur. Mingling with this came an almost tangible sense of freedom, an awareness that for the first time in her life she could please herself entirely as to where she lived and worked. Of course there was the flat, but it was only rented and could easily be disposed of, and her present job was only temporary, in a local bookshop, taken until she could find a more permanent teaching post. Now that her mother had gone, there was nothing and no one to keep her here. Tim would eventually accept that she couldn't marry him. If he still wished to keep in touch – well, that would be up to him.

The solicitor didn't keep her waiting. He was a youngish man with a computer-like brain and a conveyor-like system of dealing with his clients. 'Sit down, Miss Granger.' He was quick to wave her to a seat and even quicker to offer his condolences, the thin formality of his voice grating. Yet she found his unemotional courtesy oddly bracing, and a welcome change from Tim's well-intentioned but often suffocating sympathy. She sat down where the solicitor indicated, facing him gravely.

'I would have sent for you sooner,' he went on, his pale grey eyes sliding impersonally over her, 'but I've been out of town. Actually your mother's estate constitutes no problem, but there's something which I'm not quite clear about.'

Sue waited patiently as he paused, appearing to search for a paper on his desk. She hadn't met this man before, although she had known that her mother had consulted him once or twice, mostly about trivial matters concerning rent and such-like. She had never heard of any estate. Of course he was probably referring to the few pounds which her mother might have left in the bank. She had always used a bank account, although usually there had been very little in it. It was then that Sue remembered the insurance.

Startled, she glanced up into the solicitor's sharp-eyed face. 'There is an insurance, I believe. My father apparently had a good one and, since he died, my mother received a regular monthly sum. She never said how much. I don't suppose it would be all that much after inflation. My father died, you see, before I was born, but it was a great help – the money, I mean. I expect, now that she's gone too, that the company ought to know about it. It was silly of me not to think of it before.' Unhappy with her rather muddled presentation of the facts, and the pain it induced, Sue gripped her hands tightly together on her lap.

Frowning slightly, the man found the notes which he looked for and glanced at her keenly, his eyes resting for a moment on her pale silky head, noting the distress in her wide, clouded eyes. 'I shouldn't worry about that, Miss Granger,' he said quietly. 'A week or two is neither here nor there. Actually, though, this was one of the things I wanted to speak to you about. Your mother did mention an insurance some time ago, but when I consulted her bank I was surprised to find that, strictly speaking, there isn't any. There certainly is money paid into her account every month, but more than that I cannot find out. I wondered if you could throw any light on the matter?'

Sue started, feeling her cheeks grow cold as she stared apprehensively at the solicitor's smooth face. There was a hollow feeling at the pit of her stomach. If there was no insurance, and she saw no reason to doubt this man's word, wherever was the money coming from? 'Are you sure there's been no mistake?' she floundered nervously.

'Not possibly.' Emphatically he shook his head, waiting patiently.

Defeated she accepted this while her mind searched frantically for a suitable explanation. Her face registered dismay, followed quickly by an unexplainable fear as she found none. Intuitively she knew there was something very much wrong, but she had simply no idea what it could be. 'I only have the letter,' she whispered uneasily, speaking her thoughts aloud. Guilt surged as she mentioned it, but what else could she do?

'A letter?' A shrewd gleam lit the man's grey eyes.

'Perhaps I might see it.' He held out his hand expectantly.

'I'm sorry.' Sue flinched inwardly as she drew the letter from her handbag. 'I promised my mother I would deliver it in person and that I wouldn't open it. But if the address on the envelope is of any help, then you're welcome to look at it.' She didn't tell him that she carried it about with her all the time, almost afraid to let it out of her sight.

Gravely he took it from her cold fingers, making no comment on her odd little statement as he studied it closely. 'I see that it's addressed to a Mr. John Frazer of Glenroden, Perthshire. In your mother's handwriting, if I'm not mistaken.' Swiftly he reached for a sheet of paper, compared the two, then nodded his head, satisfied. 'Exactly the same,' he murmured, glancing briefly at Sue. 'I have here your mother's signature. This letter,' he lifted it thoughtfully, 'you have no idea what it's about?'

'No, I'm afraid not,' Sue's eyes were tensely anxious, fixed on the letter as if afraid he wouldn't give it back. 'I do intend going to Scotland as soon as possible, though, so perhaps I'll find out. Do you think,' she asked slowly, 'that it might have some bearing on this other matter, this insurance?'

'It might.' Another frown creased his high forehead. 'You don't happen to have heard anything about this Mr. Frazer, by any chance?'

As puzzled as he was, Sue shook her head. 'So far as I know Mother had never been to Scotland. We always lived in London. She used to say that Scotland was a cold, barren sort of place.'

'And you believed her?' His voice was faintly, uncharacteristically incredulous.

'Well—' Sue's pale cheeks flushed, 'not entirely. I think she might have changed her mind if she could have been persuaded to go there. I have seen films and heard other opinions. I'm only trying to explain why I find this letter so surprising. I can't think who this man can be.'

'To you he's a complete stranger?'

'I've never even heard him mentioned before.'

'And you wouldn't consider opening this letter? You don't think it might save a lot of – er – trouble in the long run?'

'Oh, no, I couldn't!' Why had he hesitated before he said trouble? He must know that he was asking the impossible. Perhaps, like Tim, he thought her too dramatic? Bewildered, she turned her head away from the solicitor's probing eyes. She had promised her mother, and a promise was a promise, no matter what the circumstances.

'I see.' He made no other comment, but she was aware that he continued to gaze at her speculatively. 'I rather think,' he said at last, 'that we will wait to see what you make out in Perthshire before we go any further. In many ways this trip of yours could be enlightening. If not – well,' he shrugged, 'another week or two can't make any difference.'

Sue still thought his remarks ambiguous as, a week later, she approached Edinburgh in the late afternoon.

'Keep in touch,' he had said, when she had rung to say she was leaving. 'Whatever you do, let me know how you get on.'

Like Tim, he had seemed quite alarmed when she insisted on going on her own, but she hadn't told either of them that her mother had begged her to do just this. Tim especially had tried to persuade her that such a course was clearly illogical, and had been quite offended when she had refused to listen to him. But this way, Sue decided as she drove along, was much better. If the mysterious letter which she had tucked away in her suitcase contained bad news, then there would be no one around to witness her humiliation. Tim never believed in restraining his remarks when time or circumstances proved him right.

In spite of the controversy about her mission, and her own inner apprehension, Sue glanced around her eagerly as her

14

small Mini ate up the miles. The car was going splendidly, something for which she was grateful. The man at her local garage had serviced it well before she left. It had belonged to her mother, who had actually bought it very cheaply with some money she had won in a competition. She had insisted that Sue learnt to drive so that they could go out together at weekends. It was taxed to the end of the year, but after she returned to London Sue knew that she would have to part with it. A car was much too expensive to run on her own, and in any case she probably wouldn't need it.

She sighed, then trying to channel her thoughts more cheerfully, thought about her journey. It had been good so far. Admittedly she would have liked more time in York. The Minster had held her enthralled, but the weather was fine and it had been no great punishment to push on. Northwards, after the industrial murk of Tyne and Tees, the hills and mountains had beckoned. There had been a short stop in the historical border town of Alnwick for lunch, then, since rejoining the A1 after her meal, she hadn't stopped at all.

Now she felt tired and as she drove along Dalkeith Road a small yawn escaped her and quickly she put her fingers to her mouth. Perhaps she had been silly to have come so far in so short a time, but there was something inside her which seemed to be driving her on, a curiosity, deeper than she cared to admit, about this man Frazer, as to who he was, and what he would look like. A curiosity curiously mixed with feelings of anger against her mother because she had never mentioned this man until it had been too late for any explanations. And obviously he must have been someone important to her at some stage of her life. Probably Tim had been right. Somewhere there might possibly be an uncle, or a grandfather maybe, whom her mother had deserted. Certainly there must be someone to have aroused such a guilty conscience. The thought that somewhere she might have grandparents living produced more mixed feelings, but resolutely Sue thrust them away, resolving once again to wait and see.

Edinburgh, grey metropolis of the North, a picturesque and beautiful city. As she arrived Sue received fleeting impressions of splendid buildings, spacious streets bordered by high tenements and narrow closes. The old and the new side by side. She progressed slowly through a heavy build-up of evening traffic, but didn't mind. Tingling interest was removing some of her recent lethargy, and anticipation grew as she gazed around, her eyes wide, each time the flow of traffic halted. Over the Waverley Bridge into Princes Street she felt a positive glow returning.

The glow faded a little, however, as she searched for somewhere to sleep. She tried several hotels suggested in her guide book without success. In the end it was only after consulting the information centre that she was able to find a room. Gratefully she took it, although it was in a more expensive bracket than what she had had in mind. She would have to economize later.

The receptionist remarked that even this one room wouldn't have been available if someone hadn't cancelled, so Sue was fortunate. 'It's because of the Festival,' she explained. 'Usually we can manage to fit people in, but at this time of the year it's almost impossible.'

Sue thanked her, making a mental note to book in advance if she should come back again. In her room she wondered uncertainly what she should wear for dinner. She hadn't brought anything very formal with her; just one long black skirt which she hadn't really expected to wear. In the end, after considering her luxurious surroundings, she put it on. With a white, long-sleeved top it didn't look exactly original, but at least she blended into the general scene. She was hungry and in a hurry and it didn't seem so very important.

Bathed and dressed, she went downstairs, for the first time since she had left home feeling a twinge of loneliness, a feeling brought on by the laughing couples and family parties around her. As the receptionist said, it was festival time and everyone appeared to be in a holiday mood. Oh, well, Sue shrugged, she wasn't here, she reminded herself, for pleasure. She asked for a quiet table and was given one by an attentive head waiter who glanced at her appreciatively. She followed him, quite unaware that in her rather severe dress, with her pale smooth hair drawn back into a velvet bow, she looked like some Victorian Miss escaped from the past.

She was half-way through her Sole Mornay when the man with the kilt came in. In Scotland now, she had been told, she wouldn't see men wearing the kilt. Tourists who expected such a sight were disappointed. Well, 'He' was wearing one! A wonderful garment in a dark, striking tartan, the name of which she couldn't begin to guess. It caught the eye, holding it, or rather the wearer did. A high, wide and handsome Highlander! Sue's breath caught tautly, irrationally in her throat. He was a complete stranger, but she had never seen anyone like him. He was tall and dark and there was assurance in every line of his well-made body, in the way he held his head. Before he sat down Sue noticed how his kilt swung gracefully from his hips.

With an effort she dragged her eyes away before he could realize she was staring. He had a companion, a girl much older than herself, but younger than the man, probably in her late twenties. One would have to reach that age, Sue thought wistfully, before acquiring such elegance. The girl wore tartan too, with a dark sash over her shoulder. They might almost have been brother and sister, as the same hard arrogance seemed to mould both their features.

Studiously Sue concentrated on her meal, refusing to take her emotional impressions seriously, relating her easily distracted mind to her recent unhappy bereavement, which must be responsible for her acting like an impressionable schoolgirl.

Then suddenly she became conscious of a pair of eyes

upon her, of a gaze so direct it could be felt, so that it drew her own magnetically. Unable to stop herself, she glanced up to find the man with the kilt staring at her, almost as she had been staring at him. He looked directly at her across the space of several feet, his eyes dwelling on her face with not a flicker of dark lashes, with a narrowed concentration, as if he were seeing a ghost.

Quickly but with a great effort, she looked away from him, a strange shudder sweeping through her, annoyed that a stranger could bewilder her with his eyes alone. An embarrassing suspicion that her own former scrutiny had subconsciously attracted his attention brought hot colour surging beneath her skin. Hating herself for being a coward but unable to trust her traitorous reactions further, Sue gathered up her belongings and scrambled to her feet. Then swiftly, without another glance towards the other table, she left the room.

In one of the large lounges she sank gratefully down into a comfortable chair, forcing herself to relax. The man had barely noticed her. She was making mountains out of molehills. Why should he notice a complete stranger when the girl by his side was perfectly charming? In any case, Sue assured herself, she would never see him again. Here, among numerous other guests and a medley of small tables and deep chairs, she would be lost and able to unwind for a short while before returning to her room. It was getting late and she would need to be away in good time in the morning.

With lessening tension she drank her coffee, then let her head fall back against the soft cushion of her chair. The lounge was quieter now, and tired from her long drive, she closed her eyes, almost falling asleep.

His voice when it came startled beyond belief, jerking her upright in sudden alarm, her face flushed with confusion.

'Good evening. I owe you an apology, I believe.' His tone was deep, totally masculine, as was everything about him. Tall and erect, resplendent in tartan, now that she was so

18

near him the impact was even more devastating than before. It was as if he had reached out and touched her physically, and fright took hold of her once again as his darkly speculative gaze met hers.

'I beg your pardon?' Gripping the arms of her chair, Sue forced the rather inane words through her lips. She could think of nothing more to say. Why should he imagine he owed her an apology? Unless . . .?

'I thought perhaps I alarmed you in the dining-room.' He continued as if she hadn't spoken, moving around in front of her, moving her coffee-cup slightly when he caught it with a flick of his kilt. Mesmerised, Sue noticed how a diamond ring flashed on one well-shaped finger. Yet all the while his eyes never left her, his stare encircled her completely, stripping her of all her assurance. Closely he regarded her smooth oval face, her fair hair, the feathery tendrils curling free at the temples, her smoky, dark-lashed eyes. 'I had a feeling that I'd seen you somewhere before. I was trying to place you, but when you left so suddenly without, I think, quite finishing your meal, I immediately felt guilty.'

'Guilty . . .?' Bewildered, Sue blinked, glancing at him uncertainly and not a little suspiciously. The man had the audacity to smile, but surely this was one of the oldest tricks in the world? He had noticed her and wanted to know her, otherwise why should a man like this stoop to such devious behaviour? It was the sort of thing one read about in fiction, not the sort of thing ever to happen to Sue Granger. For one brief, improbable moment, excitement flared, only to be as quickly squelched by common sense. Men of his calibre just didn't pick up girls like this. Nor should girls like herself entertain such wild ideas. Why he should approach her in this manner she couldn't think. Unless – her face went hot – it was as she'd thought before? He had known instinctively that she had been attracted?

Her eyes, their colour intensified by dismay, looked away from him, her clear-cut features remote. Desperately she tried to control a nervous tremor. Perhaps her best defence was to treat the matter lightly? 'I'm afraid you made a mistake,' she said coolly, after a slight pause. 'I'm quite certain we've never met before. It seems probable that you've seen someone like me. And now, if you'll excuse me . . .' She turned her head, an obvious gesture of dismissal.

Not attempting to deny her assertion, or move on, he towered above her, watching her closely, his eyes fixed curiously on her face. Neither of them heard the girl until she spoke.

Her tones laced with a faint surprise, she demanded sulkily, 'Whatever are you doing here, darling? You distinctly said you'd wait in the bar.' Her gaze dwelt coldly on Sue's taut face as she added sharply, 'I wasn't aware you knew anyone here?'

Sue, about to retrieve her bag from the far side of her chair, stopped and her head spun. The girl had approached from behind, she hadn't seen her coming. Close at hand Sue saw that her first impressions hadn't been far out. She was no teenager, but she was beautiful. Yet her face had a hardness about it which contrasted oddly with the melting softness of her eyes when she looked at the man. But Sue was certain now that she wasn't his sister. No girl would look at her brother in exactly that way.

Before she could speak the man said shortly, almost as if he didn't welcome his companion's timely interruption, 'You usually take some time to powder your nose, Carlotte. I've just been having a word with this young lady. I imagined I'd seen her somewhere before, but it seems I've been mistaken. However, as she seems to be all alone, perhaps she would care to join us for a drink?'

His suggestion did something momentarily to Sue's breath. Helplessly she glanced at the other girl, noting the frowning disbelief on her face as she stared at the man disapprovingly. In her eyes there was a clear indication that his action in approaching Sue was entirely out of character.

Sue heard her protest icily, 'But she doesn't even know us!'

'Which is easily remedied.' The man's face hardened with determination as his dark brows drew together. Politely he held out his hand, his glance returning to Sue's face. 'I'm Meric Findlay. And this lady,' his head tilted fractionally and not very kindly, 'is Miss Carlotte Craig.'

Sue wasn't greatly surprised that Carlotte didn't even bother to acknowledge the introduction. She ignored it completely, staring at Meric Findlay as if he had taken leave of his senses, her voice rising on an almost hysterical note. 'You must have forgotten, Meric, that Mother is expecting us? We're late already!'

'Then a few more minutes won't hurt her.' Dismissing Carlotte's plea, he looked back at Sue's embarrassed face. His eyes, threatening pools of cool darkness, held hers against her will.

Sue felt like a fly caught in a web, surveyed by the spider, a relentless pursuer. His dark face loomed above her, his expression enigmatic and, irrationally, her heart missed a beat. Quite without volition she felt a peculiar weakness in her limbs. The sensation was alarming, and again a small smile flickered across his lips, almost as if he sensed she was unable to move.

Then suddenly to her numbed brain and body there came a saving flash of temper. For some reason or another she had imagined that this man's curiosity might be genuine, but in an instant it occurred to her that he might possibly be using her for another purpose – perhaps to make the girl by his side jealous, or even to annoy her in some way, improbable though it might seem? Devious methods came easily to some men. Her mother had often remarked on it.

Hastily, her pale cheeks flushed, Sue rose, ignoring his hand along with his invitation as she turned to Carlotte, smiling sweetly. 'I'm sorry if I've inadvertently kept you from your appointment,' she apologized. 'But don't let me detain you any longer. I'm sure Mr. Findlay was only trying to be polite.'

Biting her lip resentfully, but the incident so far as she was concerned closed, Sue stooped to gather up her wrap, only to find that the hand which she had studiously ignored had reached down and picked it up for her. Then, with what she considered cool audacity, he draped it about her shoulders before she could protest, his fingers inflicting a tingling thrill through the thin material of her blouse. For a space of several quick heartbeats Sue paused, nervelessly, her eyes wide again as they met his. Through the ensuing silence she said, 'Good night . . .' And then, before he could reply, she fled.

Only one spark of triumph illuminated her mind as she almost ran back to her room. She had had the good sense not to tell this Meric Findlay her name.

CHAPTER TWO

THE next morning was grey and misty with a fine rain falling, drenching the spirits and clothes alike. Yet Sue felt oddly grateful for it, welcoming any concealment that a heavily overcast sky might give.

'Typical August weather!' the friendly receptionist smiled wryly, but Sue paid little attention as she quickly paid her bill before going to collect her car.

There was little to be seen of Edinburgh as she left, even the Castle was barely visible, shrouded as it was beneath a canopy of cloud. Scott's Monument stood out, registering briefly as she went past along Princes Street again, but that was all. As in York, she promised herself more time to explore on her return journey. She sighed as her foot regretfully pressed the accelerator. She supposed she was doing things the wrong way around.

Painfully aware of an urge to be gone, she drove swiftly from the city, across the Forth Road Bridge into the hills of Fife. She concentrated wholly on the wet slippery road and the water that streamed against her windscreen. Anything to keep her mind off the previous evening – the disturbing incident in the hotel. She still shuddered to think of it. Not that she could imagine ever seeing Meric Findlay again. Nor, she assured herself, did she wish to. And yet, by some strange coincidence, her heart still missed a beat whenever she thought of him, and an equally strange flicker of regret warred with her desire to forget.

Obviously Meric Findlay had been beset by regrets of another kind as there had been no sign of him at breakfast. Sue had hurried with hers, apprehensive in case he should turn up, but she need not have worried. The table he had occupied the night before was empty and there had been no

sign of Carlotte either. Sue could only decide that her conclusions had been correct. He had been using her like a small
spanner to wrest a little jealousy from his beautiful girl-
friend. People were capable of surprising things when their
affections were involved. In Meric Findlay's case the impro-
bability of such behaviour continued to tantalise, and it took
an almost physical effort to turn her thoughts in other direc-
tions, to thrust his dangerously attractive face from her
mind. She mustn't allow anyone or anything to distract her
from finding Glenroden and the mysterious Mr. Frazer.

Because of the rain and fog visibility was limited, and Sue
was thankful when at last it cleared and the sun came out.
Here, she was surprised to see that the countryside was not
particularly rugged. It was rolling country, with enormous
fields and good sized farmhouses. After Perth, however, the
landscape changed, becoming mountainous and wilder, and
after Dunkeld, where she left the main road, she felt the
loneliness of moor and forest land pressing in on her. By
consulting her map she avoided taking many wrong turn-
ings, but when she came to a village several miles along
the road she decided to stop and ask the way. She must
be getting somewhere near, she assured herself as she
parked her car outside the village shop, but she might save
herself many miles by inquiring exactly how to get there.

'Glenroden?' the middle-aged woman behind the counter
exclaimed, in answer to Sue's rather anxious query. The
shop was full, surprisingly full, Sue thought, considering the
loneliness of the surrounding country, and she felt her
cheeks go slightly pink as a dozen pair of eyes turned
towards her curiously.

'You'll be wanting John Frazer,' the woman went on as
Sue nodded awkwardly. 'Or maybe . . .'

Another woman nearby interrupted eagerly, 'I believe Mr.
Frazer has hurt his ankle. My neighbour next door was telling me only this morning. He's turned it on the heather, so
you should be finding him at home.'

Sue didn't answer but stood there silently as the two women, between them, supplied the information she needed.

'Straight on for two miles, then twice right and twice left. You couldn't miss it.'

'There are two houses, a big one and the other smaller. John Frazer lives in the small one.' The woman behind the counter glanced at Sue with a frown as she went on serving her customers. 'I seem to think I've seen you somewhere before,' she added, as she finished speaking.

'I hardly think so,' Sue replied, trying to smile as she thanked each woman for her help. Nervously she retreated to the tinkling door. 'I haven't been here before, so it doesn't seem likely.'

With a final nod she let herself out, almost running to her car, shock stinging sharply through her. She had come here looking for this man called Frazer, but to find him had crushed a slender, scarcely formulated hope that he wouldn't exist. Desperately she resisted an impulse to turn and go back home, knowing that she must refuse to pander to her somewhat cowardly inclinations. She started like a sleep-walker rudely awakened, knowing that there was one thing she must do. Any other course would allow her no future peace of mind.

Automatically her hand went out to the ignition, the sudden noise and thrust of the engine as she turned the switch jerking her back to reality. How foolish she was to sit here shaking like a leaf. All she had to do was to drive up to Glenroden, deliver the letter, then leave. Probably it could all be achieved in less than an hour, a case of simple mathematics, nothing to get in such a dither about, nor anything to justify such a predominating sense of disaster. Determinedly she straightened, brushing her fair hair back from her forehead with still shaking fingers, and drove on.

Contrary to what she had expected Sue found Glenroden quite easily. If anything her only difficulty lay in the road which twisted and turned crazily until she almost felt ill. At one spot she had to cross a ford, where a river ran over the road, and as the water surged strongly against her wheels she knew a moment of apprehension. In full flood she imagined this particular stretch of road could be dangerous to the uninitiated, and she couldn't deny a flicker of relief when she arrived safely on the other side. It would have seemed rather incongruous to have come all this way to get stuck in the middle of a stream – or should she call it a burn? It probably wouldn't matter what she called it, she thought wryly. She wouldn't be here long enough.

The river, she saw, ran into a loch which lay heavy and grey in the distance beneath the gathering clouds. Then a stretch of young conifers cut it from her view and she didn't see it again. She took the last left-hand turn, followed the river back up the glen, and found the houses she looked for half an hour later almost hidden in a circling forest of old pines.

Sue's foot jerked swiftly to the brake as she nearly missed the road end. Caught unawares, she changed gear noisily, without her usual skill, as she concentrated keenly on the glimpse of buildings through the trees. The Mini stopped dead, half tilted on the heathery verge as she turned the steering wheel too quickly.

'Damn!' She spoke aloud, but with resignation as she rested her arms momentarily in front of her. It was several seconds before she became aware of the man who stood on a rocky crag some distance away from her. It must have been a high outcrop as he stood out against the forest trees. With a sharply indrawn breath she took in the picture – a modern Turner, creating a complex scene of high drama! A vivid impression, as the great artist often gave, of energy and violence contained in controlled action, as primitive as the mountains themselves.

Although she couldn't make out the man's features, she seemed to feel his gaze upon her from his lofty vantage point. No doubt he had heard her bad change and, from his pinnacle, was pronouncing judgement. Oh, well . . . Quickly Sue looked away. What could it matter? Strangers were probably few and far between in these parts, but if he had nothing else to do then she had. Reversing off the grass, she corrected her steering and drove on. She didn't look again up to the crag.

From the moment when she drew up in front of the smaller house Sue knew that everything was going to be different. She couldn't have explained why, but she had the strangest feeling that she was coming home. The feeling persisted as she walked nervously across the wide stretch of rather unkempt grass which lay between the cottage and the long tarred drive. One wouldn't really call it more than a cottage, she decided, regarding it speculatively as she drew nearer. Maybe this Mr. Frazer was a ghillie or something like that. Certainly the house about a hundred yards further on amongst the trees seemed quite imposing. She wasn't able to see it clearly, but it did appear to be a dwelling of some size.

The door of the cottage stood ajar, something for which Sue felt immediately grateful if only because it confirmed her hopes that Mr. Frazer was at home. Tentatively, not allowing herself time to procrastinate, she knocked, but was unable to restrain a quiver of uncertainty when there was no reply. She tried again, with the same result. Then carefully, not knowing quite what to do, she gently pushed open the door and went inside.

The door opened on to a square hall, not large but beautifully panelled in a warm, dark oak. Apart from a length of Persian carpet there was no furniture, only a narrow oak stair going up from the far corner. The door on her right was closed, but the one on her left was half open, and even as she stared, still hesitant, she saw it open wide, and a man stood there.

It must be John Frazer. Sue's eyes went down curiously

27

to his foot. He hobbled, leaning on a stick. Then suddenly, with a small gasp, her eyes went back to his face, drawn there by something beyond her control, some inner conviction that she should know this man, but did not. She couldn't remember ever seeing him before.

His grey eyes were no less riveted than her own, and before she could speak he asked harshly, 'Who are you?'

His sharp direct question jerked Sue back to reality, but she was still bewildered by her own reactions. In front of her she saw a tall man whose hair was liberally streaked with grey. Fair hair, and grey eyes very like her own. Very like her own! Tenaciously the thought seemed to churn through Sue's brain as she stared, startled.

'Who are you?' the man repeated, seemingly as startled as herself, but determined also to discover her name.

For no reason that she could think of her voice faltered as she told him, unable to avoid the issue any longer, 'I'm sorry ... I should have told you. My name is Granger, Susan Granger. Mostly my friends call me Sue.'

She was not prepared for the obviously traumatic effect of her disclosure. His face went pale and his military bearing suddenly slumped, although his eyes never left her face. For a moment Sue thought he was going to fall, but as she stepped hastily to his side he waved her away. 'I'm all right,' he muttered gruffly. 'I damaged my ankle – nothing to make a fuss about. You must come in.'

Jerking out a few more stilted sentences, he turned, and she followed him across the soft blue carpet into a lounge. Unlike the hall, it was an extremely cluttered room with books and newspapers scattered everywhere, but the fact scarcely registered as she paused with him beside the open window where he continued to scrutinize her closely.

Sue stirred uneasily beneath his keen regard. 'I'm looking for a Mr. Frazer. A Mr. John Frazer,' she added nervously as the silence stretched. 'I have a letter for him – from my mother. Do you happen to be this man?'

He nodded, shock spreading with disbelief across his face, filling Sue with a confused alarm. 'Does your mother happen to be Helen Granger?' he asked, his voice odd.

Sue nodded uncertainly. 'She was.'

'Was?' John Frazer reiterated tensely. 'Do you mean what I think you mean?'

Again Sue nodded, not wishing to put it into words. She was not really surprised when he said, tonelessly, 'She was also my wife.'

But it wasn't until he actually said so that total comprehension struck. Shock flooded through her. She stood gazing at him, anguish darkening her eyes to smoky grey, her cheeks white. Was this man her father? Their likeness might be quite incidental. How could she possibly ask?

Seemingly as shocked as she was, he seemed about to say something, then changed his mind. His hand moved to her arm gently and he drew her over to the fire. 'You'd better sit down, my dear,' he said quietly, obviously taking a grip of himself. 'Before we go any further you'd better give me that letter, but I know now before I read it that you're my daughter. With your looks you couldn't possibly be anyone else.'

Numbly Sue sat in the chair opposite him in a cloud of bewilderment. Scarcely daring to look at him, she did as she was told. Finding the letter, she handed it over, some part of her mind resolving never to have it back. In retrospect Tim's warning came loud and clear. But how could she have known what she was letting herself in for? That John Frazer could possibly be her father! Just as he did, she knew beyond doubt, before the additional proof of written evidence, that he was. Rather furtively she glanced at him as he sat reading. He was tall and thin, rather frail, but over-all he looked nice, just the sort of man she had often imagined her father would be. Why, oh, why, she wondered desperately, had her mother never told her? It seemed incredible that anyone could have practised such a cruel deception or even succeeded in keeping such a thing to herself!

As for her father's part in the drama, she couldn't begin to guess. There were so many things she didn't understand. Perhaps it would be better not to try. Maybe he would try to explain after he had finished reading.

Almost as if he anticipated her thoughts John Frazer raised his head and, after another cursory glance at the letter in his hand, folded it and handed it to her carefully. 'I don't know that I should let you read it, Susan, but it might tell you a few of the things you'll have to know. Between us, your mother and I, we don't seem to have succeeded very well as parents.'

His tone was stilted as if the contents of the letter had jolted him considerably, and his face appeared drained of all colour. Momentarily Sue averted her eyes, unable to suppress the feeling that she was viewing some private bitterness, a grief which she couldn't share. Attempting to suppress her own considerable apprehension, she stared at the pages she was clutching, her eyes clinging reluctantly to the closely written sheets.

She read: For a long time, John, I've had a feeling that something is about to happen. If my intuition is correct, and it has never let me down in the past, then Susan will be left on her own. So I am sending you your daughter. If you have any doubts you have only to look at your ridiculous collection of family paintings to see who she is. I left you, John, because I never loved you, although I did try occasionally, you must admit. Glenroden was not for me, you must also admit this. And when I realized that Susan was on the way I knew I must escape. If I hadn't gone then you would never have let me go, not with a daughter or possibly a son in the offing. It was a big decision to make, but I have never regretted it.

I won't need my allowance any more, John, because if you ever read this I shall be dead. But perhaps you will keep an eye on Susan for me and, if necessary, give her a home. I'm afraid I've never been able to give her the affection she should have had. Perhaps you can supply that too . . .

There was more, none of which made much sense. Sue felt too disorganized to try and sort it out. The pages dropped from her nerveless fingers as emotion curled and unfurled inside her. The last thing she had expected to learn when she came here was that she had a father, a man who was still very much alive, contrary to what her mother had led her to believe. The news seemed more than she could assimilate immediately on top of all she had been through. She couldn't even begin to gauge the depth of her father's distress. This would probably turn his world upside down. After all, he had apparently been no more aware of her existence than she had of his. In a way – Sue put a shaking hand over her mouth, quelling slightly hysterical laughter – it all seemed too melodramatic to be true!

As if sensing her need for reassurance John Frazer said tautly, 'It might be easier, Susan, if we started at the beginning. You must understand that my surprise is as great as yours. Only I'm older, I don't shock so easily, but I must admit this seems to have rather knocked me sideways.'

Sue glanced at him a little desperately. 'If you like I'll go. You can't surely want me after all this time. I'm not quite sure myself,' she added with a sudden flicker of indignation, 'that I want to stay.'

'We can talk about that later,' he suggested with a faint smile. But his voice was firmer, and held just a thin thread of parental authority, even while his eyes stayed anxiously on her distraught face. 'I think it might be a good idea if we went through this quickly. Just the relevant facts. We can always come back to it another day.'

Recognizing the overruling feasibility of what he said, Sue shrank back into her chair, waiting submissively. His struggle to find the right words was clearly indicated by the way a frown deepened on his already lined forehead. For the first time since she had arrived she forgot her own problems to dwell for a moment on the magnitude of his, finding her heart soften suddenly at the look of extreme weariness on his face.

He rose, with some difficulty because of his ankle, and as if seeking inspiration stood with his back to the fire, thrusting the hand which was not holding his stick deep into the pocket of his tweed trousers. 'Your mother and I married, Susan, while I was in the Army. I was a second son and the Army was my career. Your mother loved the life, moving from place to place. My leaves were mostly spent in London, or abroad if we happened to be there. In those days she only came to Glenroden once, when your grandmother was alive. She didn't take to Glenroden or my mother. But I don't suppose she told you anything of this?'

Silently Sue shook her head, wholly absorbed, waiting for him to continue.

'I suppose I should have been warned, but I couldn't foresee that my brother would go before me. There was nothing I could do but come home. It seemed inevitable. Someone had to look after the estate.'

'Didn't Mother come with you?' Sue dared to ask as he paused.

He nodded his greying head. 'Yes, but she left after a short time, went to live with her mother. After her mother died she came back – I don't know why, as I hadn't been able to persuade her to before this. Anyway, we decided to try again, but again it didn't seem to work out. That last time I followed her we had one almighty row. After that I gave up. I did arrange to pay her a monthly allowance, but the last time I tried to contact her at her old home I found that she'd sold up and moved away. She never let me know where she had gone.'

'Didn't you ever want a divorce?'

'No. I did suggest it that last time, but she didn't appear to have that in mind. Or maybe,' his glance narrowed reflectively, 'it could have been because of you. As she said in that letter, if I'd known about you, things would have been entirely different. As it was,' his voice sharpened with bitterness, 'it should have occurred to me. Now it must be over twenty years too late!'

'About that,' she whispered, as he studied her soft young features darkly. 'Perhaps I shouldn't say this, but I don't think that my mother really loved me all that much. This makes what you've told me all the more confusing.'

'Your mother was inclined to be self-centred, Susan, and possessive. I suppose we all are to some extent – I don't want to start a slanging match, particularly now that she's gone. If it helps at all your fault probably lay in your looking too much like my side of the family. You are, in fact, almost an exact replica of my own mother, and every time she looked at you she must have seen it. I don't think we must blame her too much if she resented what she saw.'

Inadvertently Sue's thoughts flew to Tim, remembering his cynical observations. Quickly, to blot out the image, she asked nervously, 'Didn't you ever consider selling the estate?'

Visibly he started and she was curious to see a faint flush of colour mount his pale cheeks, a sudden wariness in the grey depth of his eyes. 'Estates aren't sold just like that, Susan. This estate wasn't entailed, but it was some years before even my brother's affairs were settled up. And then death duties took a fair proportion of it.'

His voice was steady, and the tenseness in his face had gone. She might even have imagined it. She hadn't meant to seem curious about his property, but it might prove difficult to tell him that she didn't want to talk about her mother any more. Later, perhaps, when she and her father knew each other better. Privately she acknowledged that there was still a lot to explain. He would want more details about her mother's accident, about the letter. He himself would have to confirm that the mysterious insurance had really been her mother's allowance. Relevant details would have to be sent to London, but not now. It seemed enough that she was here, and that this man was willing to accept her beyond any doubt as his daughter. A new emotion, bewildering in its intensity, flooded into Sue's heart. She didn't pause to consider that to many it might seem strange that subconsciously she was already thinking of Glenroden as home.

As if he followed and agreed with her train of thought a warm smile curved John Frazer's rather set mouth for the first time as his eyes rested, with a dawning credulity, on Sue's tense face. Before she could try to explain her feelings, he said softly, 'Why try to do it all at once, Susan? Willy-nilly we seem to have an unusual situation, and it might be better to get to know each other gradually, although fundamentally I think we both know that the ingredients for a good relationship are there. Certainly it's a rather wonderful feeling to know that I've a daughter. One can forgive much for such a privilege. I only hope, my dear, that you won't share your mother's dislike for the wilds of Scotland, as I shall certainly expect you to make your home here.'

Not wishing to lose her somewhat precarious self-control, Sue nodded speechlessly. His words affected her strangely as she became aware of the perceptiveness behind them, a thread of sensitivity which she had found inexplicably lacking in her mother's make-up. Taking a deep breath, she glanced away from his gently tired face. 'I might even be able to help you run the estate,' she said.

'The estate ...' His voice went tight, the tenseness returned. His weariness was suddenly, curiously cynical. 'I have a partner, my dear, a very able man. I don't somehow think that he would appreciate your help. He takes care of everything nowadays – saves me a lot of time and bother, leaves me time for my own pursuits.'

'But surely,' Sue stared at him, her smooth brow creased, 'you must still have a lot to do. I mean ...' confused, she groped for the right words, 'you must have to supervise everything?'

Evasively her father replied, 'Actually, Susan, I'm writing a thesis of Army manoeuvre from 1745, a bit before your time. There's a deal of research involved and it keeps me busy. Of course I do get around the estate from time to time.'

Sue's smoky-grey eyes were puzzled and, though common sense warned it was irrational to pursue the subject, something tenacious inside her wouldn't allow her to leave it alone. 'This house,' she gazed around her, impressions, ideas piling and merging in her over-taxed mind. 'I suppose you once lived in the other one which I saw through the trees, and it got too big for you?'

'Why don't you tell her to mind her own business, John, instead of standing there looking helpless!'

Sue jumped, literally, in her seat, a wildness invading her eyes as she heard that voice. It thundered with open menace, telling her quite clearly that he was her enemy! How long had he been standing there? Her pulses stopped, then shuddered. She didn't need to turn around to see that he was the man in the hotel – and the man on the crag. He was Meric Findlay!

'It's all right, Meric.'

As she swung around John spoke, confirming her suspicions, although she seemed unable to hear anything clearly above the hammering of her heart. His forcefulness hit her like a blow as his eyes leapt over her full of inexplicable derision. Stunned, she could only stare. Evidently he regarded her as an enemy. It was much worse than his bewildering behaviour the evening before. Then his antagonism hadn't been quite so obvious.

John Frazer glanced swiftly from one to the other, vaguely puzzled. She could see it in his face as he turned and sat down again in his chair. Pulling herself together with an almost visible effort, she said coldly, 'I think Mr. Findlay must be jumping to the wrong conclusions. I would even go so far as to say that he could owe me an apology.

35

Unless, of course,' her chin tilted contemptuously as her smoky eyes met his dark ones, 'he can produce a logical explanation!'

'Sue! Just a minute!' her father interrupted with frank astonishment. 'I think I'm the one who needs an explanation. You two apparently know each other, although I'm sorry you don't appear to be on the best of terms.'

Meric Findlay cut in ruthlessly, 'I met this girl only last night, John, but I knew at once who she was.'

'She happens to be my daughter. You couldn't possibly know that.' John's eyes flickered with growing perplexity.

With dark eyes narrowed Meric Findlay ignored Sue's wrathful face. 'She didn't say who she was, John. I still don't know her name, but I could see by her looks that there was some family connection. I was convinced that she would arrive here today, and I haven't been proved wrong. In fact I saw her coming. If I hadn't been up on the Crag I might have been here in time to stop her.'

'You did hear me say she's my daughter, Meric?' John broke in with quiet insistence, oddly defensive.

'I don't care who she pretends to be,' Meric Findlay said dryly. 'Just so long as you don't believe her without proof. You're too vulnerable, John, always have been. I don't care how many odd relations you collect, but don't ever say that I didn't warn you!'

Sue's blood boiled as her eyes came alive with a helpless kind of anger. No one had ever spoken to her like this before and she found it totally unacceptable. This man considered her an impostor, but, even if he had been right in his assumptions, it certainly didn't give him any right to be so rude. She winced almost aloud as she deliberated on his attitude. He had been more than ill-mannered. He had been devastating, clearly bent on destroying a relationship which might as yet be too fragile to withstand the onslaught of his calculated attack. And, if the glint in his eyes was anything to go by, he was obviously enjoying his campaign of destruction! There was a slight tremor in Sue's voice, but she managed to look straight at him as she retorted hotly, 'I can assure you, Mr. Findlay, that my visit here was, to begin with, a mere formality. That John Frazer happens to be my father was as great a surprise to me as it obviously is to you. And as to whether I stay or not, that can't possibly be any of your business!'

There was complete silence as she finished speaking. His eyes still holding hers, he crossed the room to rest his weight on the edge of the cluttered table. The glint in his eye had developed into a positive glitter, and she could almost physically feel the impact of his unyielding personality. She might have been a fly which he was preparing to swat at his leisure, as his eyes travelled over her from head to foot full of cool derision.

'But you have decided to stay, have you not, Miss – er – is it to be Frazer?'

'Of course she's going to stay, Meric,' John Frazer injected stoutly. 'If you'd just hang on a minute until I explain . . .'

'Of course she's going to stay,' Meric Findlay repeated sarcastically, his eyes turning to John Frazer as if Sue didn't exist. 'She'll stay until she decides whether she likes it here. And if not, she'll be trotting straight back to London.'

'I would not!' Stung beyond control, Sue jumped furiously to her feet, ignoring her father's plea for rationality as indignation bubbled over inside her. She could at least cope with her own enemies, and if she was to stay here, it might be better to start as she meant to go on. Certainly she didn't intend to be dominated by Meric Findlay. As she stood near to him it didn't help to see herself reflected in his sardonic dark eyes, or to feel so ridiculously small beside his large bulk. But what she lacked in stature he would find she made up in temper! John Frazer was obviously overruled by this man. Turning to glace at him as he sat anxiously back in his chair, Sue knew a faint prickle of irritation that this should

37

be so. 'Do you always let your manager dictate to you like this?' she accused, sparks flying from eyes curiously now more blue than grey.

'Susan!' There was a moment's electrified silence. Sue flushed, her temper suddenly fading. It seemed that she had committed the unforgivable, and must apologize. But before she could do so, her father added, his face paling strangely, 'I told you before, Susan, that Meric is my partner.'

'Oh, well,' Sue's long lashes blinked uncertainly, 'it's all much the same thing, isn't it? And,' she added bleakly, still looking at her father, 'I'm sorry if I've seemed rude, especially as I've just arrived, but Mr. Findlay hasn't been exactly pleasant himself.'

The observation did not go unheeded. Mr. Findlay replied coolly, with a wry twist of his firm lips, 'She could be right, John. Instead of indulging in a slanging match it might be better if Susan and I agree to a truce, juvenile though it seems. No doubt there'll be plenty of time for explanations later. I do know that you've been married, John, so it seems quite feasible that you should have a daughter. We'll leave it at that for the time being and concern ourselves with arrangements for tonight.'

Slightly dazed by his change of tone, Sue stared at him wordlessly for an instant. Why should he worry where she spent the night?

'I'm afraid I haven't made any arrangements,' she admitted tonelessly. 'But I'm sure it must be possible to find accommodation in the village. I didn't realize it was so late.'

John Frazer interrupted abruptly. 'Of course you can't go to the village, Susan. From now on your home is here, with me. I don't want to lose you just when I've found you.'

Sue's heart was suddenly heavy with remorse. He looked tired and frail. The news which she had brought here today must have been disturbing, even though he hadn't seen her mother for many years. She knew a sudden urge to stay to look after him. And surely he must need someone, living here, as he did, all on his own? If only Meric Findlay would disappear instead of towering over them with that superior expression on his face, then perhaps they might get something sorted out.

But it was not to be, although for a moment, as he stalked to the window and stood there framed against the sunset sky, she thought he was about to depart and leave them in peace. Instead, after a brief contemplation of the weather, he turned back, his eyes narrowed over them.

'There's no room here, John, for Susan to stay, and you well know it, but there is plenty of space up at the house. Your own room will still be aired from last week, and if we go now we might just catch Mrs. Lennox. She'll soon fix something up for Susan.'

'Please.' She looked at him uneasily with troubled grey eyes, but his hard, handsome face didn't soften. Instinctively she was aware that he was used to getting his own way and, when he dictated, men usually ran to do his bidding. Well, here was one person who would not! She glanced away a little wildly from his dark, taunting eyes, but not because she was frightened of him. If he wanted a fight then she was more than prepared to give him one. He certainly wouldn't find her as docile as her father.

She drew a long quivering breath. 'If this cottage has to be good enough for my father, then it's good enough for me. I'm sure I'll be able to find somewhere to sleep without troubling your Mrs. Lennox.'

'John!' Impatience tightening his voice, Meric Findlay swung grimly to his partner. 'Won't you please tell this girl that I have enough to do without wasting further time! The rooms upstairs are used as attics, junk rooms, stuffed full of your things, and your one bedroom across the hall isn't much better. It would take a month to clear them out, and I haven't time to stand here arguing!'

It annoyed Susan that her father did exactly as he was told. 'It would be better, I think, my dear. To stay here wouldn't be very feasible. You see, I use this house more as a retreat, while I'm busy writing. Since my last housekeeper went I haven't bothered very much. I'm afraid I rely too much on Meric.'

Which was very obvious! Sue fumed inwardly. He was clearly under this man's thumb, but was it necessary to be so humble? Surely as owner of the estate it was he who ought to be giving the orders? Maybe it was her duty, if only for a short while, to stay, to help him reassert himself against this self-proclaimed dictator. And maybe in the big house she might be in a better position to put Mr. Findlay properly in his place before she left!

She looked at him quickly, her voice silky soft, her cheeks defensively pink. 'If it pleases my father, then I'll do as you suggest. But just so long as we can come back here eventually. I shouldn't like to be beholden to you for too long, Mr. Findlay!'

CHAPTER THREE

AWAKENING in her huge canopied bed next morning, Sue
allowed herself the luxury of an extra ten minutes to lie and
think. The weariness of the previous evening had disappeared, and her eyes were wide as she gazed around the large,
well furnished room, feeling that she might almost have to
pinch herself to believe that she was here at all.

Her bedroom was truly mediaeval, or so it seemed to Sue,
used as she was to modern apartments with their slick, built-
in cupboards. The furniture around her couldn't have been
changed in a hundred years! Huge dark wardrobes, a wide,
brass-handled dressing table; even a washhand-stand complete with china basin and jug, all edging the faded square
of unwear-outable carpet, all made to last another hundred
years at least! Sue had never seen such furniture outside
the country houses which she had occasionally visited –
after paying the requisite fee. She had certainly never
envisaged staying in one, if only for a few nights.

Curiously she wondered if the rest of the house would be
like this. She had only seen the kitchen the night before.
Before leaving the cottage, while John Frazer collected a
few things together, Meric Findlay had rung the big house,
and when they arrived Mrs. Lennox had supper already
waiting. Then she had gone to get Sue's room ready. Sue
had actually eaten by herself on a corner of the kitchen table.
Her father, complaining that his ankle was extremely painful, had decided he would go straight to bed, if Sue would
excuse him. Meric Findlay had disappeared with him, not
returning until Sue, having finished her meal, had left the
kitchen in search of Mrs. Lennox. Half dazed with tiredness, she had stood uncertainly outside the door, not knowing which way to go. She had scarcely been aware of

someone striding into the hall until he stood beside her.

He had given her a steady look, his dark eyes watchful.

'John's room is along the hall,' he had told her smoothly. 'Third door on the right. Do you want to see him before you go upstairs?'

'Yes, of course,' she had stammered, unnerved by his steely glance, and quite unable to meet it fully. In spite of all that had been said she had known that she was still a stranger. She might have found a father, but as yet knew no great affection for him in her heart, and the thought of going with Meric Findlay to say good night filled her with an incomprehensible dismay.

'It's not so easy, is it, Miss Susan?' His stare had been as disconcerting as his words. Words which he had used bluntly, with little sympathy for her newly discovered uncertainty.

'How could it be easy?' she had flung at him with tired indignation. 'If you were aware of the facts, then perhaps you might understand.'

'Oh, John did explain quite a lot as I helped him settle in,' he assured her mockingly. 'It's not beyond comprehension. But you're beginning to find, are you not, that facts and emotions are two different things?'

'You could be right.' Reluctant as she was to concede him even this one point, Sue's voice had been little above a whisper.

His eyes had narrowed sharply on her tense face. 'If I were you,' he'd suggested, 'I'd look at the situation through the eyes of a child viewing a foster-parent for the first time. Then you might not feel so distracted.'

'But with foster-parents there are usually no – well, blood ties.'

'Which doesn't always count half as much as we like to think. It's often the associating ties which are more important. You and your father haven't any of these as yet. Maybe you never will.'

42

She had stumbled away from him then without replying, hating him a little for his cruel remarks while unable to deny the veracity of them. He might have succeeded in clearing a degree of confusion from her mind, but she didn't like him any the better for it. 'Say good night to him for me, please,' she had whispered, half over her shoulder as she had run clumsily upstairs. This morning she couldn't somehow remember whether he had answered her or not.

She could scarcely remember getting into bed. Dimly she did recall how Mrs. Lennox had whipped off her clothes with seemingly practised hands, having her between the sheets in minutes. 'You'll feel better tomorrow, dear,' she had smiled, glancing intently at Sue's tired face. 'I've been a nurse and I should know. Mr. Frazer has been telling me the news and I'm delighted. Delighted, too, that you're so pretty. I've often wondered what you would be like.'

Strange words, now that she came to consider them, totally inexplicable. Sue frowned, then shrugged her bare shoulders impatiently. Mrs. Lennox must have a lot to do, and had probably just phrased her thoughts wrongly. Anyway, she could ask her later, after she had had a cup of tea. An unfamiliar longing for one made Sue wonder about the time, and as she groped around for her watch, she remembered also that Mrs. Lennox had added before she went that she wouldn't be here today. Whatever else that might mean it certainly seemed clear that she wouldn't be around with any early morning tea. In any case it was after seven and she must get up and see how John Frazer was feeling.

But before she could move there came a knock on the door, and before she had time to even acknowledge it the door opened and Meric Findlay strode into the room. Utterly surprised, Sue had barely time to pull a sheet up to her chin before he seemed to be towering over her, thrusting a cup of tea on to her bedside table.

Vaguely, in the midst of turmoil, Sue heard herself thanking him as his eyes raked over her stunned face. His glance

43

was compelling, impaling her against her pillows as unmercifully as a butterfly on a pin.

Hardily he disregarded her tentative thanks, not beating about the bush as his eyes met her dilating ones. 'You'd better drink that quickly. Mrs. Lennox isn't here, and your father isn't well. And, as you're partly responsible, I'm afraid you'll have to help look after him.'

Unnoticed, the edge of the sheet escaped Sue's nerveless fingers as his words jerked her upright, exposing the taut lines of her slim young figure beneath the thin silk of her nightdress. 'How do you mean, not well?' Her voice managed to be almost as sharp as his as she stared back at him in consternation. She ignored her tea.

He picked it up again, forcing her to take it. 'Get it down,' he said curtly. 'You still look washed out. I don't want two invalids on my hands. I do lead a fairly busy life, and all this feminine dithering is time-consuming.'

Almost choking, yet disconcertingly aware of his dominating authority, Sue did as she was told. She had been about to refuse, then changed her mind. Perhaps if she obeyed he would explain and go. The exploratory inventory of his eyes affected her strangely. Panic was hidden beneath her cool reply. 'I'm sorry if I'm wasting your time, but why should you hold me responsible for my father? His ankle, I believe, was hurt before I arrived.'

'It's not his ankle. It's his heart.' He spoke abruptly, without expression, but leaving her in no doubt as to the authenticity of what he said. 'The doctor came last night, after you'd gone to bed.'

'You should have told me!'

'Why?' Scornfully he dismissed her exclamation. 'What good would it have done? I'm used to John's attacks, and you'd had about all you could take!'

So he had noticed? Somehow his noticing removed a little of the chill from around her heart. Not that he was sparing her now! Half desperately Sue's hands tightened around her

44

cup as she gazed at him, mute inquiry in her eyes. 'He might have died!'

'One of these days he might.' He refused to give her the reassurance she unconsciously sought. 'Some things are occasionally beyond the power of human administration, as Doctor McRoberts will no doubt explain. And if it's explanations you're after you might be interested to hear that apparently the good doctor has known all about you from the beginning.'

'From the beginning?'

His eyes narrowed with bewildering inconsistency on her breathlessly parted lips. 'If you're always going to repeat what I say it might go to my head. Especially if you continue to look at me as you're doing now.'

'Oh, please . . .' Colour splashed her pale cheeks as she became aware of the subtle punishment which her constant interruptions inflicted. The sudden glint in his eye reminded her that he was very much a man who, if tried too far, would not allow their short acquaintance to deter him from seeking greater penalties.

But then he shrugged, and she went cold again as he said, 'It appears that your mother consulted McRoberts years ago, before she left Glenroden for good. John, I'm afraid, doesn't seem to appreciate that, bound by medical ethics, McRoberts was unable to tell him about his own child, but maybe you can make him see reason.'

'Mrs. Lennox said . . .' Totally disorganized, Sue stopped half-way, completely incapable of digesting what he told her, her mind swinging inexplicably back to the evening before.

'Well, what did Mrs. Lennox say?' he prompted smoothly, as she made no attempt to finish, but sat staring at him like a bewildered child.

Uncertainly Sue blinked, her eyes unseeing on his hard, handsome face. 'Something about having wondered how I would turn out. How could it have been possible for her to have known? I thought I must have heard her incorrectly.'

'Not necessarily. Mrs. Lennox used to be the doctor's receptionist and nurse, before she married and moved away, I believe. The information would be down in the surgery files.'

'Now she's back?'

'Yes, but not with McRoberts. He's had someone else for a long time. Besides, she's a widow now, and not so young as she used to be. She has a cottage and helps here. Her nursing experience is useful when John isn't well.'

There was a short, tense silence as Sue's mind sifted and tangled with the information. Nothing seemed crystal-clear, but one fact seemed to stand out as her clouded vision sought for clarity. 'It seems beyond doubt that I am Susan Granger-Frazer?'

He smiled thinly. 'Quite conclusively. I'd drop the Granger bit, if I were you. It's not relevant any more.'

She said unevenly, 'I'm not quite sure yet what I'll do. You knew who I was at the hotel?'

His eyes were suddenly guarded. 'Let's just say that I knew you were a Frazer, and knowing about John's heart I was alarmed. And I think for the time being we'll leave it at that, Miss Susan. Right now I'm going to suggest you get out of that bed.'

The hardness was back, arousing her resentment, making her aware that Meric Findlay could be more of an enemy than a friend. The brief and obviously senseless but dangerous attraction she had felt for him in the hotel was gone, and she knew a flash of relief. He might have relieved her mind about certain things, but she refused to let even a flicker of gratitude show through. Rebelliously, her chin lifted slightly. 'As soon as you're out of the room,' she said softly, 'I shall do as you suggest with pleasure.'

It seemed to Sue to be hours later before she had time to draw another breath. As she washed and dressed quickly her

46

thoughts veered inconsistently from her father to Meric Findlay. Meric Findlay, she decided, was someone whom it would be wiser not to trust, and whom, in her father's interests, it might be better to investigate. It might seem impertinent as well as mercenary to seem too curious about her father's affairs straight away, but it was something to bear in mind. A little bit of private sleuthing as she went along couldn't do any harm. Since her father's health had broken down he had probably left everything in this man's hands, which wasn't a good thing. Well, now he would have someone of his own to help. Mr. Findlay might be a sort of partner, but woe betide him if he took so much as one step out of place! If she hadn't found it possible to love her father yet, then there were other ways of proving herself a dutiful daughter.

Bolstered a little by her brave if highly impractical thoughts, Sue scrambled into a cotton dress, brushed her hair haphazardly with one or two sweeping strokes, then ran downstairs.

There was no one about and she was glad that she knew where to find the kitchen. But with one hand on the door she hesitated, her eyes going to the huge grandfather clock in the hall. It was after eight. Perhaps she should go and see how her father was – if he needed anything? Undoubtedly Meric Findlay with his sweeping efficiency would have taken him a cup of tea, but that might have been some time ago.

Still nervous, she almost tiptoed back along the hall, counted two doors and knocked gently on the third, remembering what Meric Findlay had told her. When there was no reply she carefully turned the knob and looked in, almost ashamed of her relief at finding John Frazer fast asleep. The room had obviously been turned into a bedroom. It was comfortable, and warm from the small fire which burnt in the hearth. Her eyes returned to the man in the bed. He looked exhausted, and had probably had a bad night. She felt an unusual stir of pity in her heart as she studied his

47

worn face, and vowed again to help him all she could.

A tray with the remains of a light breakfast was on the table by his bed. Maybe Mrs. Lennox had popped in for an hour or two after all? Swiftly Sue picked up the tray, closing the door softly behind her as she went back to the kitchen.

As soon as she opened the kitchen door Sue knew there was someone inside, but her eyes widened to see Carlotte Craig sitting by the window, very much at home, drinking coffee! Since she had never expected to see Carlotte again, or quite so soon, surprise held her silent while the girl looked her coolly up and down.

'I shouldn't just stand there if I were you,' Carlotte drawled above the rim of her cup. 'Come in and close the door. You seem capable of worming your way into most places.'

Her voice was insolent, her eyes as unfriendly as they had been in Edinburgh, and her choice of words clearly reflected her frame of mind. Sue was hungry and didn't feel particularly friendly herself, but a flicker of curiosity controlled an equally sharp reply. How had Carlotte known she was here? And why was she here herself? She must surely live somewhere in the neighbourhood to be here so early. Obviously, as on their previous meeting, Carlotte resented her. But why? Was she already engaged to Meric Findlay, and considered Sue an interloper?

Slowly Sue placed the tray she was carrying on the wide scrubbed table, wishing fervently that she was more familiar with the general layout of the kitchen. She couldn't very well start searching for things while Carlotte sat surveying her with such a cool, calculating stare.

'Were you seeking Mr. Findlay, or did you come to see my father?' she asked, a hostile urge to make Carlotte aware of her own position warring with her usual leaning towards politeness, so that she tempered the impact of her words with a slight smile.

But if she had hoped to startle Carlotte then she was to be

disappointed. As if she had seen quite clearly through Sue's subterfuge, her thin lips curled contemptuously. 'I met Meric on the glen road, and he was telling me you're claiming to be John's daughter. I simply couldn't resist the temptation to come and see for myself. I am, by the way, John's cousin.'

'John's cousin?'

'Yes. People do have cousins, you know. And my claim might be much more authentic than yours.'

'What do you mean?' As she met the animosity in Carlotte's eyes, Sue's voice was little above a whisper.

'I mean . . .' there was a furious clatter as Carlotte jumped to her feet, leaving her cup on the window-sill, 'that in spite of what John or McRoberts say – or what ever Meric chooses to think – I intend to expose you, even if it takes months!'

Sue sat down abruptly, feeling the strength drain from her legs as Carlotte slammed out without a backward glance. She knew a growing desire to follow Carlotte, to pack her case and never come back. If this house had been so full of intrigues when her mother lived here, then no wonder she had run away. With unseeing eyes Sue stumbled to the window, resting her hot forehead against the cool pane, immediately regretting her hasty thoughts but unable to control them.

Then, lifting her head a little, she looked down the glen. Before her it spread into the blue distance, barely touched yet by the first warm tints of autumn, but full of promise of the vivid colouring which would surely come. Already the heather was purple where it covered the rough, undulating ground against the bare mountains. Last night in the dusk there had been mist on the hills, but this morning the contours stood out, clearly defined against the skyline. Water glinted, catching the sunlight where it ran through rock, and over the lower slopes came the dark green frosting of forest.

A land enticingly beautiful. Sue's breath caught in her

49

throat and, for a minute, she forgot Carlotte's threatening words. The willow trees against the low stone wall outside bent gently to the warm west wind, beckoning her to come and explore. Suddenly she longed to be out, flying through the heather, up into the woodlands, into the world she could glimpse at through the trees.

But of course she could not, though how her mother could have left such a place she could not think. With a sigh she turned from the window and, as she did so, her eyes fell upon a note propped between a teapot and a jug of milk. Slowly she walked across to the cabinet where the teapot stood. The note was addressed simply — Susan, and nervously she picked it up. The handwriting was masculine and before she opened it she guessed it was from Meric Findlay. It was, and he wrote,

'I wouldn't advise you to disturb John. He'll probably sleep until lunch time when Mrs. Lennox could be back. Just look in now and then to see if he's O.K. I won't be in for lunch, so don't start preparing anything for me.'

The note terminated abruptly and, equally, abruptly was signed Findlay.

Thankfully Sue put it down, unable to suppress a flicker of relief that she wouldn't see him again for at least a few hours. It would give her time to rally her defences, and, she thought wryly, to try to find some food for herself. He talked of lunch while she hadn't even had breakfast yet! With an indignant hand she swept the remains of his from the kitchen table, carrying the empty dishes to the sink.

When at last she did find something to eat Carlotte's strange behaviour kept spinning through her head, and suddenly she wasn't hungry any more. With a frown she pushed aside her last piece of toast. If Carlotte was really John's cousin and expected to marry Meric Findlay, then she might also expect to inherit the whole of Glenroden, and if the size of the house was anything to go by then the estate itself must be quite large. By coming here Carlotte probably saw her as a threat to all her plans, and, if she was entirely mercenary, no wonder she was bitter.

Sue sighed worriedly, losing interest in her breakfast as she jumped to her feet and started to tidy the kitchen. Anything was better than sitting bothering herself with things which must have happened before she came here. There must be plenty to do. The intrigues of Meric Findlay and his girl-friend would have to wait until she had more time to consider them. But, unaccountably, as she worked her heart ached with a peculiar pain as she pictured Meric on the glen road that morning telling Carlotte all about her.

To her relief Mrs. Lennox arrived back before twelve, earlier than Sue had expected. 'I managed to postpone my second appointment, dear,' she smiled. 'I thought it best, as everything here will be strange to you, and Mr. Findlay would be too busy to show you around.'

Gratefully Sue returned her smile. John hadn't woken up, but he had been restless, and Sue had felt a guilty apprehension each time she had peeped into his room.

'Sometimes he sleeps for hours,' Mrs. Lennox assured her, 'when he's ill like this. I'll look after him now that I'm back. I know exactly how to go on. But that isn't to say, dear,' she added, 'that he won't want to see you when he does wake up. In fact it might be better to stay near at hand, as I'm sure you'll be the first person he asks for.'

Sue nodded, and helped Mrs. Lennox to prepare a light lunch before accompanying her on a tour of the house.

'I don't rightly know if it's my business to do this,' she confessed, as they progressed from room to room. 'The trouble is I'm never quite sure where the Major really lives. Whether it's here or down at the cottage.'

'The Major?' Puzzled, Sue looked away from the wide precincts of the drawing-room to gaze inquiringly on the nurse's bright face.

'Your father, of course. Didn't you know he was in the Army? The regulars, that is.'

'Oh, yes.' Understanding dawned as Sue turned her head. 'I didn't know his rank.'

'Never mind.' Quietly Mrs. Lennox closed another door and beckoned Sue back to the kitchen. 'It doesn't really matter. You can't find everything out at once. How do you like the house?' She changed the subject abruptly.

'It's nice . . .' Then, because that sounded insipid, Sue smiled warmly, her small even teeth gleaming white. 'I didn't want to say, but it's just the sort of house I've always dreamt of. Big, but not too big. Comfortable without being dreary. Full of antiques which manage to look beautiful as well as old. The whole atmosphere is somehow nice.'

Mrs. Lennox nodded approvingly as she stoked up the boiler. 'I've felt it myself. It's a pleasant house. Mr. Findlay thinks so, too. He's bought some of the nicest antiques himself, over the years. Perhaps he'll show you some time when he's not too busy.'

'Mr. Findlay would appear to be a very busy man.' Unaware of the hardness of her tone, Sue avoided Mrs. Lennox's inquiring gaze, her mouth set mutinously. 'I suppose,' she conceded, when Mrs. Lennox didn't reply, 'that when my father is ill he has everything to do himself.'

Which wasn't exactly what she'd meant in the first place, and she knew that Mrs. Lennox knew it!

To Sue's dismay John Frazer's attack turned out to be a bad one, and it was several days before they were able to have much of a conversation. During this time she hadn't ventured far from the house, but could find nothing to verify her own suspicions. Although Carlotte was around quite a bit, fussing over-loudly about her cousin, Sue didn't notice that Meric was over-attentive, but then he wasn't the type to wear his heart on his sleeve. He could be spending quite a lot of time with Carlotte for all she knew. Somehow she had a feeling that Mr. Findlay, in spite of his enigmatic exterior, was no hermit. There was something about his mouth which made her suspect that he enjoyed a little dalliance with the

52

opposite sex, even though she herself did not arouse his interest. Nor, she assured herself emphatically, did she want to.

She couldn't deny, however, that even if he seemed generally unaware of her existence she was very much aware of him as a man. She saw little of him. During the day he was seldom in for meals, and in the evening he often went out for dinner, apparently not eager to share a simple repast at the kitchen table. But something about him, each time she saw him, drew the same response which she had been vividly conscious of in Edinburgh. It was probably just those ridiculous kilts which he wore, she decided wryly. In them he looked like some wild Highlander from one of her father's books. Reason enough for any girl's heart to miss a beat, but no grounds whatsoever for imagining that she was irrevocably attracted.

But her heart continued to annoy her by behaving unpredictably one evening when he did come home early. Mrs. Lennox usually went back to the village for an hour or two each night before returning to sleep in case she should be needed. It was quiet, and after dinner Sue sat for an hour with her father, then left him happily studying a huge military tome which Carlotte had brought. She always seemed to be bringing him something, and not always, Sue thought privately, were her gifts very suitable. Not that she ever openly objected as John seemed to welcome the girl, and her gifts gave him much pleasure. Indeed, Sue sometimes thought herself that she might have misjudged Carlotte if it hadn't been for the occasional glances she intercepted. Secretly Sue suspected that her frequent calls had as much to do with Meric Findlay as her father, but it would have been unkind to say so.

On this particular evening a peculiar restlessness made it impossible for Sue to sit still any longer, and after assuring herself that John's bell was within reach, she gently closed the door and wandered into the drawing room. She was standing gazing at a painting of her grandmother when Meric Findlay walked in.

He didn't surprise her as she had heard him moving in the hall, but her eyes swung, startled, as she saw who it was, silently berating her sixth sense for not warning her. At this point she had known there could be no escape. Not that this mattered, she told herself stoutly, yet somehow wishing that he hadn't caught her staring at a family portrait.

'You're home early?' She uttered the first thought to come into her head, a sudden confusion drying her lips. Cautiously she wetted them with the tip of her tongue, embarrassingly aware of his dark eyes on her mouth as she did so. Hastily, when he didn't speak, she tacked on, 'Have you had dinner?'

'I've had dinner, thank you.' His hard face closed up, inscrutable. Yet something about her naïve little speech appeared to amuse him – or was it her appearance? His eyes roved slowly over her, taking their time, indifferent that they subjected her to a disconcerting scrutiny.

The silence didn't seem to bother him, if indeed he noticed it. His eyes probed, exploring each detail of her figure, the fine, clear outline of her face, her hair baby-fine, yet heavy, curving on to her shoulders, returning to her eyes, the beautiful clouded grey which contrasted so softly with a gardenia-pale, rose-flushed skin. He seemed bent on a minute examination, and Sue's body tensed as a flickering flame shot through it.

Then suddenly, as his eyes left her, swinging to the painting on the wall, she understood, and his next words confirmed her conclusions, subduing the turmoil in her heart.

'No one could ever deny you are a Frazer,' he said slowly. 'But how much of your mother is hidden beneath the outer shell, I wonder?'

His eyes were hard again, and his voice, following the theme, had a deeply cutting edge. A disparaging inflection.

Why should he disapprove so of her mother? He hadn't known her. Why then should he sit in judgment in this lordly fashion? Loyalty dies hard, even harder than affection, if Sue had stopped to consider. Instead she tumbled headlong into the trap. 'You probably don't mean to be insulting!' she retorted with an angry little gasp.

'Knowing the circumstances one could scarcely be anything else,' he answered with a cool detachment which she envied. 'When a woman denies a man his own child she can't expect the world to judge her kindly.'

'But she was only one side of it, wasn't she? Perhaps if my father had cared enough to retain some form of contact, if . . .' Her voice tailed off weakly, her doubts and fears clearly reflected in the extreme sensitivity of her face.

He said brusquely, his eyes unfathomable as sickness held her, 'I shouldn't lose any sleep over it if I were you. You could console yourself that you were too young to know anything about it. Very few of us are granted such immunity from the mistakes of others.'

The extreme dryness of his tones taunted her. He was a mocking devil, careless that his words hurt as he jerked her body and mind alike. Her head spun as she went helplessly lax. The numbness of the last weeks had been like an anaesthetic. Now feeling returned, yet with a curious emptiness, as if the whole of her unconsciously yearned for some new experience beyond her reach.

She stared at him, desperately frightened, not knowing if she could cope with the enormity of her reactions, knowing she must have time – if only so much. And because she knew that in some way he was irrevocably bound up with these feelings she over-reacted like a distracted child. Unwilling that he should guess that he disturbed her, she disregarded his advice with resentful stubbornness.

Recklessly blind to the glint in his eye, she said, 'You talk as though divorce and separation are irrelevant in this day and age. What, I wonder, would you have done if your wife

55

had left you like that?'

The glint in his eye deepened as he regarded her small defiant chin. 'I should see to it that she never wanted to leave in the first place, but we didn't happen to be discussing me. You missed the point at the beginning, my dear Sue. I only intended advising you against leaving Glenroden, should you entertain such an idea. I merely suspected that you might share your mother's tendencies to run at the wrong moment, and that would never do.'

He couldn't actually be threatening her? Tautly her slim white fingers went to the low neck of her dress, hiding the nervous pulse at the base of her throat. 'You mean because of my father?'

'Another shock wouldn't help him.'

'Like – when I came back?' She moved away from him then, alarmed by his cruelty, her eyes resting momentarily and blindly on her grandmother's face, unwilling to admit the logic of what he said, waiting tensely for his reassurance.

But none came. Only his hands came up behind her as she turned, gripping her bare arms, the steely strength of his fingers hurting. Yet he held her impersonally, as if he was shaking a dense child, his voice terse in her ear. 'If you like. But for heaven's sake don't torture yourself, girl. It's just not the time for soft words, if that's what you're wanting.'

For a moment her lips parted wordlessly as, while mind tussled with body, she slumped back against him. Then, with an almost frantic effort, she wrenched herself free, whirling to face him, the imprints of his fingers red on her upper arms. 'I just wouldn't expect any kindness from you, Mr. Findlay. Why should I? And you might be my father's manager, but you certainly aren't mine! Whether I go or stay is none of your business. Please remember that!'

Furiously Sue heard her own voice, slurred and choked with emotion as she almost ran from the room. With a little more dignity she might have given the impression that she had had the last word, but not now.

It seemed equally perplexing that she should feel curiously restless and unsettled during the next few days. So much so that Mrs. Lennox noticed and advised her to go out for a change.

'I'll pack you a few sandwiches, dear. You can take your car and explore, then have your lunch. If you keep to the road you can't go wrong. You could go to the loch and the air will do you good, bring a little colour back into your cheeks.'

She had promised to keep an eye on John, but it was reluctantly that Sue went. Although he was now getting up daily, Doctor McRoberts had warned her not to let him do anything, just gentle exercise around the house. Today he had seemed tired and said that he would stay in bed. So at least, Sue thought wryly, as she reversed her Mini from the garage, she knew where he was.

Once out on the road she felt her spirits lifting and was glad she had taken Mrs. Lennox's advice. She hadn't realized it would be so good to be out. A still autumn silence lay over the moors, broken now and then by the abrupt firing of distant guns. John had told her only that morning that Meric took shooting parties out two or three days a week at this time of the year. Sue had been surprised until he explained in detail.

'It used to be my thing,' he had smiled wistfully. 'I stopped holding shooting parties myself some years ago, but we have an arrangement with the hotel in the village. We provide the shoot, and they provide the shooters. It involves quite a bit of hard work, taking everything into account. I don't know how long Meric can keep it up, but it certainly helps, financially.'

'How long has he been with you?' She hadn't meant to ask, but since that night in the drawing-room Meric Findlay had never been far from her thoughts, even if, as she tried to persuade herself, it was only because of his questionable activities.

John had glanced at her quickly, as if he found the wording of her question curious, but all he said was, 'About ten years. He came here in his middle twenties, and had a lot to learn. We sort of helped each other, if you know what I mean. His father died in South Africa, so he had no one else.'

Sue didn't know exactly what he meant. She was fast learning, however, that when asked to be more explicit he often recoiled into a sort of shell from which it was difficult to prise any explanation. Instead she had concentrated on the South African bit, sudden interest surging through her. But before there had been time to say anything Mrs. Lennox came in, and she had decided to leave it. It would keep until another day.

CHAPTER FOUR

DETERMINED not to dwell any longer on that which worried her, Sue concentrated on finding the loch. Mrs. Lennox was a trained nurse; her father would be in good hands. Yet in spite of her former resolutions Sue frowned. Was it natural at her age to find all illness tedious? Secretly she was ashamed to admit it. Her mother's attacks of migraine, whenever anything upset her, had been trials to be endured, involving as they had done long periods when the slightest noise had been taboo, when even the sound of Sue's transistor turned low had been forbidden. It didn't help much to remember how her occasional resentment had usually propelled her to her mother's side with extra assurances of sympathy. If Sue had ever thought of a father, he had always been a particularly robust figure. While John Frazer pleased her intellectually, his frailness, due to his heart condition, dismayed her. And again, as with her mother, a guilty conscience plagued her unmercifully.

With little difficulty Sue found her way, back over the river ford, taking the right-hand fork instead of the left which would only take her to the village. The Mini was going well. Woman-like, she had worried that there wasn't enough petrol, but the tank she could see was half full and she recalled filling it up after she had left Edinburgh. The weather was good today, and the countryside enticing, and on the road the dark-eyed sheep scattered before the car. Huge boulders dotted the landscape with hidden crevasses, while rough grass and heather encircled bare slabs of rock. Ideal spots for a dry picnic, she noted as she drove on, not really keen to stop until she reached the loch.

She was not really surprised to pass several cars. After all, it was the tourist season. She remembered that first day and all the people in the village shop. Even so, these roads were deserted compared with similar roads in the south. The south . . . Suddenly she wondered if she would ever go back. Did she really want to? It might not be altogether easy to stay here. It would be foolish to think so. She would have to make new friends, eventually find a job – she couldn't just wander around Glenroden for the remainder of her days. Her heart gave a downward jolt. If Meric were to marry Carlotte Craig she might not be able to stay here at all.

Then, around the next bend, without warning she came upon the caravan site. Protected, and almost hidden, by a screen of birch and conifers, it stood well above the loch on a flat green plateau, but within easy reach of the lapping water. Startled, Sue pulled off the road on to a wedge of tarmac, and stared. It was one of the nicest parks she had seen, yet a niggling resentment bothered her. It seemed an intrusion on her privacy. All around the mountains and wild, lonely places were at their best, basking in early autumn sunshine, and here was the very thing she had hoped to escape from – crowds of people!

Driven by some inner compulsion, not because of inclination, Sue left her car to walk down the wide track between the vans. She saw a notice which said clearly: Glenroden Caravan Site. No vacancies. She didn't attach any particular significance to it. It was only when she saw Carlotte coming around the corner of one of the caravans that suspicion began to grow.

Carlotte stopped, obviously as surprised as Sue. 'Whatever are you doing here?' she asked, her eyes wary.

'Having a look around,' Sue stated, none the less bluntly. Which wasn't quite what she had had in mind, but Carlotte shouldn't ask silly questions. Besides, why should Carlotte act as if she owned the place? Surely – the thought struck Sue from out of space – surely she didn't live here? Suddenly she realized she had no idea where Carlotte lived. She had imagined in the village.

'I'll show you around, if you like?' Smoothly, a cat with the cream smile on her face, Carlotte waved a magnanimous hand towards the park, taking little notice of Sue's raised eyebrows.

'Show me around?' Deviously Sue sought to satisfy her curiosity. 'Why should you do that?'

Too easily Carlotte saw through her. 'If you mean, do I live here, or own the place, then the answer is no. It belongs to Glenroden.'

'You mean, the estate?' As she asked Sue flushed hotly. She hated having to persist. Why had no one told her?

It didn't help that Carlotte nodded her sleek dark head, her stare superior. 'It seems there's a lot of things you don't know about. I wonder why?' While her words were innocent enough her tone was mocking. 'The woman who usually sees to the office is away for a few days, so Meric asked me if I would help out.' Her tone, shifting slightly, implied much more than that.

Slowly Sue froze. Unpredictably her heart lurched downwards again. The two of them, in it together! What did they need with a caravan site at Glenroden? Surely an estate of this size needn't resort to this? 'My father didn't mention it,' she replied stiffly. 'But then he's ill, and I don't see a great deal of Mr. Findlay.'

No sooner was it out than Sue regretted the last bit of information. A smug smile spread over Carlotte's mouth. 'Meric wouldn't wish to discuss these things with you,' she said, 'especially as you're a stranger. He doesn't think you'll stay long, not after John's better, so he would only be wasting his time.'

With difficulty Sue restrained a biting retort. Carlotte might be speaking the truth – she wouldn't put remarks like that past Meric Findlay – but she was obviously baiting her. She must refuse to be antagonized. Then she might find out what was going on. She bit her lip sharply, then releasing it, smiled. 'I think I would like to see around if you don't mind.

Now that I'm here.'

The next hour she spent with Carlotte, walking around the park. It was a good one; she soon realized that. Every mod. con., even a small shop where, as Carlotte explained, such necessities as milk, bacon and eggs were sold. 'Other items can be bought at the village shop,' she told Sue. 'This site has helped them quite a lot.'

The caravans were all occupied, she added, as people liked it, and its reputation in the last two years had spread. And the holiday season now stretched well into the autumn. In fact this was fast becoming the most popular time of the year.

Their tour over, she invited Sue quite cordially into her office for coffee. Sue thanked her and accepted, feeling it would be churlish to refuse after the time Carlotte had spent with her. Carlotte, she thought wryly, would have made a good courier for a travel agent. She appeared to excel at this sort of thing. If she was trying to demonstrate her usefulness to Meric, then she had certainly succeeded.

The office was small and well equipped. Carlotte eased her elegant, trouser-suited figure into a comfortable chair behind the desk, waving Sue to the seat opposite. 'Another woman will be along in an hour or two to release me,' she said. 'The busiest times are early morning and after tea, when new people arrive. Meric doesn't expect me to cope with those.'

Which could mean many things, Sue grimaced cynically, a short time later, as she drove away. Either Carlotte wasn't as competent as she appeared to be, or Meric Findlay was over-solicitous for his lady-love. She went on, around the loch where she stopped to eat her lunch in the middle of the afternoon, but somehow, for some inexplicable reason, she hadn't the heart to explore further.

'I've had quite a nice day, though,' she assured Mrs. Lennox, who looked at her searchingly, obviously puzzled by her early return. 'I'll take tea in if you like, then you can get away. Perhaps I remembered that you need time off as well as I do.'

Picking up the already prepared tray, she went along to her father's room, resisting an impulse to ask Mrs. Lennox about the caravan park, afraid that she might get another answer such as Carlotte had given her. It might be better to tackle Meric Findlay himself, when she next saw him.

Then, with a start of surprise, as she opened John Frazer's door she found Meric with him. As she entered he rose, he took the tray from her and placed it smoothly on a small table by the fire before turning, his eyes narrowed on her suddenly flushed face. 'I believe you've been out?'

And he wanted to know where she'd been — if she interpreted his tone of voice correctly. Well, his curiosity could remain unsatisfied for a few minutes. She smiled briefly at her father before answering with a question of her own. 'You're back early. Where is your shoot?'

'In the capable hands of my second in command. I hope.' His voice was light and taunting, as if he guessed her intention to procrastinate and was willing to go along with it — so far. 'When I left they were almost through, and will probably be back at the hotel by this time.'

'You can obviously dispense with your duties lightly, Mr. Findlay.' With uncontrollable antagonism she gave him back look for look. Their eyes clashed, his a shade dangerous, hers glittering like sparkling ice.

'I think,' he said, hard and deliberate, 'that wherever you've been the air hasn't agreed with you, Miss Frazer. But I'm sure your father would appreciate his tea more than your temper!'

Mortified for a moment, her hands clenched tight, Sue glanced towards the bed, relieved to see John leaning close to the radio and Gardener's Question Time. Her head came up proudly as a faint remorse left her. Someone had to put this man in his place. Her father apparently couldn't care less. She moved away blindly to the fireplace and started pouring tea, her lashes dark fans against her cheeks.

Meric said nothing for a long moment as she attended to her father, but his silence offered no comfort, totally more threatening than mere words. As she passed him a cup – Mrs. Lennox always put a spare one on the tray – she flicked him one apprehensive glance, then just as quickly looked away. Today he wore his usual kilt and tweed jacket. Beneath this he wore a tan shirt and a plain tie, and at his waist, hanging from a strap and chain, was a brown leather sporran. A sporran, she knew, was necessary because a kilt has no pockets. Stockings he wore of tan wool, with garter flashes, plus heavy brogues. In the top of his right stocking she noted a horn-handled knife in a scabbard. His knees were vagrantly exposed. He looked hard and handsome, not willing to concede an inch.

Her stormy eyes flashed over his wickedly sardonic mouth and she bit nervously into a cucumber sandwich. 'When I was out,' she announced sharply, 'I discovered, quite by chance, a caravan park down by the loch. Carlotte kindly showed me around.'

There! At last it was out, laced, in spite of herself with angry reproach, and as she said Carlotte's name, an upsurge of unfamiliar jealousy. Immediately she felt Meric's quick glance, her father's slightly disturbed one.

It was her father who spoke, with faint agitation. 'I've been ill, Susan. These things slip my memory.'

Meric added with intense irritation, 'Why make an issue of it, Sue? Apart from being ill, your father doesn't care much for caravans en bloc. In the first place, I'm afraid the whole idea was mine, so perhaps it's quite natural that he forgot to mention it.'

'There are other people in the house besides my father!' Too late Sue was aware of her injured tone of voice, the flickering resentment in her wide eyes.

His dark eyes explored her own, totally objective, wholly provoking. 'Other people happen to be busy, my dear.'

64

Colour flooded her cheeks. 'Meaning that I'm not?'

His face darkened and for a moment she thought he was going to cross the room and shake her. He looked a stranger, dark and formidable. 'On the contrary,' he spoke coldly. 'But our affairs scarcely lie in the same direction.'

She ignored that with feminine logic. 'You can't possibly work every evening. You could have spared a little time to put me in the picture.'

Disturbingly the heavy mouth twitched a little at the corners as his dark eyes rested on her.

'If I could be sure you would find my company entertaining, Miss Frazer, I would be more than willing to oblige.'

That he meant something quite removed from what she had in mind seemed obvious. His eyes, directly meeting her grey ones, were filled with clear menace, something for her to ponder over. Until you're ready to meet me half-way, keep your distance, they seemed to say. Completely shattered by her own crazy interpretation, Sue cried unwisely, 'There's no reason to suppose that Miss Craig monopolizes all your free time!'

The glint in his eye deepened at that into clear hard laughter. 'You might tell your daughter, John, how I spend most of my evenings. Dining at the hotel, in the interests of business.' He ignored her reference to Carlotte. Seeking her father's support might be relevant, but seemed purely incidental.

Mumbling, John stirred himself from his preoccupation with his tea and radio, only half aware of their verbal sparring. 'Should have been my job, as I told you, Susan. A lot to discuss of an evening. Used to be a most enjoyable part of the day – in the old days, when people stayed at the house . . .'

Inwardly fuming, Sue bit her lip, which seemed to be becoming a habit. Her father and Meric together were like a stone wall and, in their different ways, equally impregnable. She could never hope to make headway against their combined forces. Driven by a helpless frustration, she said scornfully, 'It's surprising what goes on in the interests of business.'

There was a silence. John, refusing, perhaps owing to the nature of his illness, to retain any prolonged interest in anything which worried him, retreated to his radio, turning up the volume, leaving the issue to Meric, ignoring Sue's indignant face. So much registered with Sue before her eyes left him to collide once again with Meric Findlay's dark ones. He was finishing off his tea in one deep draught, his glance still on a curious level between anger and amusement.

Putting his cup back on the tray, he stood up, his forcefulness hitting Sue like a blow. It drove all the nervous reaction from her body and for several seconds as she braved his dark eyes, she regretted her hasty words. Picking up her own cup in order to brace herself against further reprisals, she took a distracted sip.

When he did speak his tone of voice deceived her for a minute. He said softly, 'I don't ordinarily go round explaining my actions, Miss Sue, and I don't intend to start now. If you have in mind a private investigation, then you'd better start conducting your own.'

'I wasn't . . .' she choked.

'Wasn't casting aspersions?' His voice, silky smooth, slewed over her. 'Wasn't that what you had in mind? Rather an old-fashioned way of putting it, but nothing more original could be so apt.'

Sue flushed, colour creeping vividly beneath her skin. Never in a hundred years could she hope to make headway against such a man. His voice, sardonic, drawling, taunted her more by its inflection than his actual words, but his mind was razor-sharp and she wasn't at all sure that she liked it. Defensively she flung fretful fingers across her brow. 'You must admit that I'm entitled to be told more? My father is ill; I can lay no blame at his door.' Desperate to break an inner tension, she glanced pleadingly towards her father.

He had finished his tea and was fixing one of his cheroots, taking his time over the clipping and trimming and lighting. He surprised her by saying through the trail of blue smoke, 'Meric came home early today to show you around. You've been here some time and lately he's been of the opinion that you might like to see something of the countryside.'

'That wasn't quite what I meant.' She stirred restlessly, startled by what he said, yet only faintly mollified as she looked at Meric again. 'I'm not just a passing tourist and to be treated as such. To discover something by chance can put me in an embarrassing position. Carlotte at the caravan site, for instance. It was rather humiliating having to confess I knew nothing about it!'

From his great height Meric looked down at her, his eyes ironical, a hint of mocking despair in their dark depths. 'A Scottish glen, especially a Perthshire one, is full of all sorts of enticing things – woods, hills, moors, rivers and streams, rich in wild life. And out of all that you have to find a caravan park!'

So she had been right about the laughter. Her voice was dry as she retorted, 'You're convinced that a city-dweller's intuition led me to it? A sort of magnetism.'

He taunted, 'Or an inborn curiosity, which isn't particularly prevalent in towns. As for Carlotte, she isn't above helping me out, should I ask her nicely. And she does have all the information any holidaymaker might need, as well as being charming.'

With a sharp twinge of shock, Sue stared at her hands. He found Carlotte charming! The knowledge struck her, irrationally painful. She took a deep breath. 'If I stay I, too, might learn to be useful.'

'Not at the caravan park, if that's what you mean.'

'Not exactly ...' Her voice trailed off, her confused thoughts defying clarification. The emphatic tightening of his hard mouth didn't help or she might have told him she had no wish to remain here as an outsider. Mutinously she shrugged, her eyes going slowly to the patch of bare skin which showed between the bottom of his kilt and the top of his stocking. The skin was tough-looking and firm, like the rest of him; dark brown in colour, weathered by the winds. Suddenly she knew a crazy longing to touch it and, as impulse surged, her pulse jerked and she swiftly looked away.

A piece of coal falling from the fire made her aware of his waiting silence. Hastily she picked up the tea tray and scrambled clumsily to her feet, not attempting to finish off her sentence but starting another. 'Perhaps I owe you an apology, Mr. Findlay. If you did intend to show me around, then I'm grateful, but I'm afraid it's much too late. You may not be aware of it, but I usually cook dinner. I'd be perfectly willing to go another day.'

But another day didn't arrive too quickly. Meric Findlay, in fact, appeared to forget all about it, and Sue, although eager to be shown the estate and the exact boundaries, was reluctant to remind him. Probably, she decided, as manager he was hesitant about making the first move, but that she seemed unable for some indefinable reason to make one herself proved a bit of a dilemma.

Helping Mrs. Lennox about the house kept her occupied to a certain extent, but not nearly enough. Yet her father still had bad days when he needed both of them. Even so Mrs. Lennox did all the nursing and Sue was determined that as soon as he was really better she would see about a teaching job. Locally, some authority somewhere must need an infant teacher. It might be a good idea to make a few inquiries. According to her map Perthshire abounded in small villages.

She started with Mrs. Lennox. 'I'm sure I wouldn't know, dear,' the woman replied when she asked. 'They've had the same two teachers at our village school for years, and neither of them is old enough to retire.'

Sue frowned. 'I might have to go further afield.'

'You might.' Mrs. Lennox hesitated, noting Sue's serious expression. 'I should wait until your father's fully recovered, though. He seems to worry when you're out of his sight, and anything like what you have in mind might upset him.'

'Of course,' Sue's reply was perfunctory. How could she explain to Mrs. Lennox she wouldn't mind staying forever if only she could feel that she was really a part of Glenroden? Her father clung to her because he was thrilled with his new-found daughter, and the idea of introducing her to his friends when he was stronger pleased him. But she wanted to be more than a show-piece. She wanted to belong! Would anyone here really miss her if she was gone?

She said, her mind switching erratically, 'Mr. Findlay might be glad to have me off the place more often. He must get tired of having me constantly underfoot.' Which was a devious way of seeking reassurance in a certain matter, but suddenly it seemed important.

Mrs. Lennox's eyes rounded with genuine surprise as she glanced at Sue. 'I'm sure you're mistaken, dear. I don't suppose he often notices you're here.'

Sue's eyes gleamed with derisive amusement. Well, she'd asked for that! Not exactly the answer she had hoped for, but one which she no doubt deserved. Yet she persevered if in another direction. 'Carlotte must still be at the caravan park,' she went on. 'She hasn't been here for some time. I asked Father where she lived, and he said near Perth, so she must have a good way to travel.'

Mrs. Lennox nodded absently as she started to prepare lunch. 'Her father, who was your father's first cousin, is dead, and she lives with an elderly relation on her mother's side. I think she was the only relation your father had until you turned up.'

'Mr. Findlay seems to like her . . .'

'I expect he does, dear.' Sue suspected that when Mrs. Lennox chose, she could be deliberately obtuse. 'She does come a lot to Glenroden, and they've always got on well together.'

Sue turned away as her father's bell rang. She wasn't going to get anything out of Mrs. Lennox. To be at Glenroden was like living in a vacuum. The past and future could apparently have little bearing until her father was up and about, and until then she was caught in a prison of her own making. If she was aware that most of her strange restlessness stemmed from an entirely different source she refused to admit it. Meric Findlay had no part in her future plans whatsoever!

One evening, after dinner, she decided to go down to the cottage. As usual Meric was out, but Mrs. Lennox was there, not having gone home that afternoon, and Sue thought it an ideal opportunity. To pass the time she had been helping John research his book, and over the last few days they had both been immersed in the Jacobite rebellion. John had fought Culloden in at least three different ways, and had now passed on to the Hanoverian army of occupation.

Sue's help was invaluable, he pointed out, as, once he was well, he could find in her notes all he needed to complete his thesis. His first rough notes, still at the cottage, he asked her to fetch. There was also two books with additional information which he would like to have by him. Not bothering to put on a coat as the late September night was still warm, she picked up a basket to put everything in, and let herself quietly out by the side door.

The cottage, some distance from the rambling old Georgian house by road, could be easily reached by following a grassy track through some trees. To Sue's dismay the night was already beginning to darken as she hurried along the path, although the setting sun enhanced the beauty of hill and glen, slowing her flying footsteps in spite of herself. She liked the smell of autumn woods, the sweet aroma of grass drying out, a ripening reflected in the red of the rowan berry; the darker purple of the blackberry; the gold of the hazel-nut. Other things changed, but not these.

Quickly she unlocked the cottage door, cross with herself for lingering until she realized that the electricity supply had not been cut off during John's absence. With a flick of her finger the little hall flooded with light, but she switched it off again. It wasn't yet dark enough to need it, and she had promised herself a quiet look around. If someone saw a light they might come to investigate.

Rather furtively she explored the little house, finding everything much as Meric Findlay had described it on that first evening. Faintly disappointed, she returned to the living room and set down her basket on the still cluttered table. She had asked John several times about coming back to live here, but in every instance he had only looked put out and shook his head.

'I thought you were comfortable here, my dear,' was his usual reply. 'I've only been using the place to write in since my heart started to play up. Meric doesn't care for me being there alone.'

'But you've got me now,' Sue had argued. Secretly she was beginning to get fond of the big house, as everyone called it, but Meric Findlay disturbed her, and some instinct of self-preservation warned her to move before it was too late.

Her father, however, was adamant. 'You're not aware of all it would involve, Susan. Think of all the renovations which would be necessary, and which you couldn't hope to cope with yourself. We're much better off where we are.'

Which was a matter of opinion, but now that she had seen for herself Sue could understand his point of view. The upstairs rooms, though structurally sound, were chaotic, with bits of plaster and wallpaper peeling. Stuffed full of junk, they would take a week to clear out. The other room downstairs had obviously been used as a bedroom, but here again it was untidy and smelt musty. It was perhaps difficult to understand why her father had come to live here in the first place.

71

Once or twice she had tried to broach the subject, but he seemed to find it difficult to talk to her very deeply about anything, apart from his book. Although he had promised to stop her mother's allowance at the bank, he appeared reluctant to discuss anything else. In the end she had had to write to the solicitor in London herself, giving brief details and a promise to keep in touch. Which reminded her that she had also promised to write to Tim. She had sent him a short note soon after she had arrived. It must have stopped him worrying, but he would be waiting to hear further. It was rather surprising that he hadn't replied. He must be waiting cautiously for further details which, because he had always been so good, she must supply.

Carefully she searched amongst the array of writing material on the over-burdened desk. Finding what she required, she removed the pen and pad to the table and sat down to compose a letter. Reluctantly she picked up her pen. Conscience dictated that she wrote straight away, while she remembered, but over the last weeks Tim seemed to have receded into the background and she scarcely knew where to start.

'Dear Tim,' she wrote at last, 'You will be surprised to hear that my father owns a large estate . . .'

No! Dissatisfied, she stopped, nibbling the end of her pen. That sounded — well, ostentatious? Frowning, she reached out to tear up the page and start again when a sound at the outside door made her jump. Someone was there. Could it be Mrs. Lennox seeking her? Was there something wrong? Instantly she was on her feet, alarm spinning her to the inner door, only to find it flung open in her face as Meric stood there.

'Whew!' she gasped, half in relief. 'I heard something and thought it might be a ghost.'

'A ghost would scarcely have given you a whiter face,' he said dryly, closing the door behind him before gripping her arm and guiding her to the nearest chair. Bending down, he switched on the fire. 'A disused room gets cold,' he informed her. 'A little heat and you'll soon recover.'

Sue thrust the thought from her that it was much nicer to bask in his solicitude, much more warming than a mere fire. Instead she protested weakly, 'There's nothing wrong. I just didn't expect to see you, that's all.'

The look he slanted her was oblique. 'You never do, do you, Sue? I might be wholly flattered if I thought for a moment that I was responsible for all this feverish activity!'

Her lashes fluttered as she tried to sustain his ironic stare, colour creeping like wild rose beneath her skin. Retreating a little, she lay back in her chair, unable to fight against his hard masculinity. She tried to concentrate on what he said. 'I thought perhaps it was Mrs. Lennox with bad news. I suppose it was foolish of me.'

'Very.' He didn't pretend to misunderstand her, and suddenly it seemed his eyes were kinder. 'Actually I didn't find you by accident. John told me where you'd gone and I decided to come and walk back with you. It will soon be dark and you might get lost. Besides, I had something to ask you.'

Only half hearing, Sue gazed at the flickering fire as a dozen muddled emotions went through her. She was scarcely aware when he turned and sat in the chair opposite, where her father had sat that first evening. What could he want to see her about? Nothing of importance, surely. In a moment of nervous panic she spoke. 'I'm helping Father with his research – which is really why I'm here, if he didn't explain. I'm to find him two books.'

'It doesn't bore you?'

'Why should it?' She inclined her fair head as she straightened and her hair fell in an arch across her flushed cheek. 'I must admit,' she confessed, 'that I wasn't quite sure when I started, but I'm getting more interested every day.'

'You're interested in Scottish history, or is it the way John

73

fights every campaign as if he'd been there personally?' There was a glint in his eye again. He could be teasing.

She replied lightly, 'His strategy seems good. Bonnie Prince Charlie might have fared better if Father had been there. As for my interest? Well, after all, Scotland is my country, even if I've just found out.'

'I haven't been long here myself. Only, in my case, I came back.'

'You came back? You mean,' Sue glanced at him sharply, 'you'd been here before, on holiday?'

'Not exactly,' he drawled cynically. 'I don't suppose John got around to telling you, I left with my parents when I was six. My father was a bit of a gambler, not a soldier like yours.'

'A gambler?' Curiosity flickered through Sue's grey eyes, and Meric's mouth twisted with obvious amusement.

'There are many kinds of gambling, Sue. He gambled everything he had and I suppose it paid off, but he lost his life.'

She glanced at him, startled, meeting the cool level gaze. Breathlessly she asked, 'What did he really do?'

'Gold-mining.' He didn't add anything else.

'Oh, I see . . .' She didn't like his harder expression.

'No, you don't, but leave it. Sufficient to say that I returned.'

'But you must have lived in South Africa a long time,' she persisted. 'Didn't you mind leaving?'

'If I had I shouldn't have left. I had only myself to please. Maybe I felt the pull of my native land. How about you?' Lazily he stretched his long legs to the fire, subtly diverting her interest in his own affairs. 'You've lived in London all your life, yet I take it you don't miss it too much?'

'Not really . . .' Uncertainly Sue paused. It seemed a ready-made opportunity to ask his advice about the flat, and it was inevitable that she asked someone. It wasn't a decision she felt free to make herself. Meric Findlay, in spite of his

74

derogatory remarks about her deserting when he had found her in the drawing-room, was the obvious person to ask. He had been with her father for years and, in the circumstances, must know him much better than she did. Making up her mind, she said quickly, before she could change it again, 'It's the flat. I'm not quite sure what to do with it. If I let it go I'm not likely to find anything so reasonable. Finding anything at all is very difficult.'

He flicked her an odd look, his eyes narrowed. 'So we're back to that again. You want to go home.'

It was a statement, not a question. He had already come to his own conclusions. Anger slipped through her, reflecting in her eyes as they met his dark ones. 'You deliberately misunderstand! You enjoy judging me without knowing any of the facts. You must realize that I had to live somewhere before I came here. My mother and I had a flat. Someone she knew let her have it cheaply, or cheaply perhaps compared with prices here. The lease still has some time to run, but that isn't the problem. When I left it was merely to deliver a letter. I intended to return and find a teaching post.'

'That isn't a problem, either. You could easily find such a job around here,' he said dryly, his eyes as wary as her own.

'That's not the point!' Wildly Sue felt like tearing her hair, but he only laughted hardly.

'You could try explaining exactly why you want rid of that lease but daren't let it go.'

'Oh, don't be absurd!'

'I'm not being absurd,' he pointed out calmly. 'But until you're willing to elucidate more clearly, my remarks might continue to infuriate.'

'I was leading up to it!' Defensively, her cheeks pink, Sue dropped her eyes from his to stare down at the fire again. Her hair fell across her cheek and she thrust it impatiently to one side. Did he expect her to throw all her half-formulated fears in a heap at his feet? She had only asked about

75

the flat. Not for an inquisition!

Confusing her still more, he leant forward, his hand shooting out to grasp her wrist. 'I wouldn't want you to strain those ingenious resources of yours, Miss Frazer. You just take your time. While you're thinking about it I might well pass the time making us a nice cup of coffee. The ingredients will all be in the kitchen, right down to the powdered milk.' He grimaced, shrugging his wide shoulders as he released her hand and stood up. 'We might reach some sort of understanding before midnight, but that's up to you. I'm not in any hurry.'

CHAPTER FIVE

Sue rose to her feet and followed him into the kitchen, her wrist still tingling where his fingers had gripped, the sensation, illogically disturbing, running up her arm. Every instinct cried out against having coffee with him here in this old cottage where it was so easy to whip up an atmosphere of intimacy which she wished to avoid. She was too aware of Meric Findlay not to realize he could be dangerous, although, she decided wryly, she was probably insane to imagine that he had any personal interest in herself.

On her round of exploration she had missed the kitchen and she saw now that it was small, more of a kitchenette, something like what they had had in the flat. In the confined space two people could scarcely move without touching and she gazed around, pretending curiosity, but only conscious of the man by her side. There was in the sardonic gleam of his dark eyes, that which dared her to retreat. She didn't even dare a murmur of protest about coffee.

Which left her no good reason for being there. Confused, she sought to explain her presence in another way. 'I asked Father about coming back to live here, but he doesn't seem to keen. I can't really understand him.'

Meric removed his narrowed glance from her face, turning to the cooker with the kettle he had just filled, striking a match as he switched on the gas before settling the kettle on the naked flame. 'Does that mean,' he asked softly, 'that you don't care for living with me?'

At this Sue looked up, startled that he had applied his own interpretation, uncertain that she agreed with him, yet unwilling to concede even an element of doubt. 'You're quite wrong,' she retorted over-vehemently. 'As we scarcely see you I don't know what put that into your head!'

77

'You don't claim any responsibility?'

Was he alluding to his frequent absence, or the latter part of her statement? Refusing to be drawn, she rejected his remark as nonsensical, and went on, 'I really would like to live here, but he won't even discuss it.'

He lifted his head from the stove and looked her full in the eye, his voice on a thin line of patience. 'I've told you before to give him time.'

'You mean to recover?'

'Not exactly.' He spoke flatly, as Sue might have done to one of her own pupils. 'It's a big thing for him at the moment to come to grips with the past. Living with me, at the big house, he doesn't feel committed to anything.'

Sue frowned, her smooth brow wrinkling, not fully understanding although she wanted to. In retrospect she considered her father's behaviour. 'On his good days he sometimes takes me to see my grandmother's portrait in the drawing-room, almost as if by comparing the two of us he can convince himself that I am his daughter.'

Meric passed her a jar of instant coffee. Opening a cupboard, he took two mugs from their hooks, putting them on the sink-unit as she unscrewed the top of the jar. Silently he handed her a spoon. 'You're trying to say that he doesn't attach any reality to you?'

'If you like to put it that way.' Carefully Sue measured out two spoonfuls of coffee. 'I know he doesn't love me, not yet anyhow. I know he likes me, and has some sort of family feeling towards me, but that's all.'

'And you expect more?'

She tried to speak more boldly, but her voice quivered. 'I don't expect anything. I had hoped, maybe, but I don't honestly know how I feel myself.'

His eyebrows lifted, creasing his brows in a way she found disconcerting, while his mouth quirked resignedly at one corner. His patience, it seemed, was being tried a little. 'Listen, Sue, it might be better if you looked at the whole

78

thing from this angle. Remember what I told you when you first came? Think of yourself as an orphan, a foster-child, and be content to let your relationship with John develop gradually. If you like each other, then you've got a good base on which to work. But for heaven's sake get rid of all these guilty feelings of inadequacy.'

Sue's face registered bewilderment rather than conviction. 'The trouble is I'm not a child. Besides, children usually accept situations without curiosity, and I'm afraid I can't do that.'

He returned her gaze with long-suffering endurance. 'So there are things you want to know. Well, fire away, but don't be too disappointed when I don't know the answers.'

'Thank you,' she said, with a matching irony. 'I didn't make a list. Just the odd thing, perhaps. What my father is really like – deep down. It might be a whole lot easier if I knew.'

'Why?'

She hesitated, conscious more than ever of the rock-like arrogance in his face. His eyes held hers, making it impossible to look away. Nothing could be easy beneath that intimidating stare. Stumbling, she attempted to put into words thoughts which she had always kept hidden. 'My mother . . . She never believed in showing her feelings. I can never remember her giving me a hug, or showing any affection, not towards me or anyone I ever knew. It might sound ridiculous, but sometimes I used to think she was partly frozen, incapable of being warm and outgoing, all the normal, natural things a mother ought to be. But I don't seem to be making much headway with my father, either.'

His head went back as comprehension dawned, yet his eyes lingered sardonically on her taut face. 'And you can't let it go. You've got to delve and dig and dissect, and now you're wondering if you've inherited adverse characteristics, maybe from both of them? What you've got to get into that beautiful head of yours is that experiences such as your parents went through invariably leave a scar, but not one which need necessarily affect their offspring. What makes you think that you're cold by nature, not capable of all the normal responses?'

She drew back startled from the gleam in his eye, her pulse jerking. 'You aren't much help, are you! I was only pointing out a possibility.'

'And I was merely pointing out that you seem quite well adjusted to me. If you must pursue the matter further, then there are questions you must ask yourself. How do you react when a man makes love to you, for instance? I couldn't possibly know the answer to that one.'

Mockery had replaced the even keel of his voice, and Sue flushed scarlet at the bluntness of his words. 'I don't know what you mean,' she spluttered, knowing very well what he meant but unable to confess, when it came to the point, that she had never known any wild thrill when a man had kissed her. Did that amount to coldness?

His gaze moved wickedly over her face. 'I could demonstrate, if you like, but you might not approve of my methods.'

'Oh!' Sue felt the colour deepen in her face as he left her in no doubt of his intentions. Still full of nervous confusion, she turned her head. 'I think we're talking about two entirely different things.'

'But each of which is irrevocably bound up with the other, my little coward.'

A minute ago she had trembled when he said she was beautiful. Now he called her a coward. She drew back, her eyes fixed on his face, widely resentful, the thick lashes flickering. 'I don't agree. I wouldn't have mentioned the subject at all but for the fact that my problems don't just concern me, personally. I don't want to hurt anyone else.'

Those dark eyes examined her face again, and suddenly the kitchen was too small. Heat swept up through her body and, unconsciously, her hand went to her shirt neck, undoing the top button so that the skin of her throat gleamed smoothly white. She had a frightening feeling that she was suffocating. If she had hoped to receive rational advice then she had obviously approached the wrong person. There was no help here in the indolent tilt of dark eyebrows, the mocking speculation in equally dark eyes.

'I don't think you can be a bit like your mother,' he drawled, blocking the entrance to the kitchen effectively as if he guessed her desire to escape. 'Quite clearly, in spite of her failings, she must have been a person of decision, which you're not. You want someone to make yours for you all the time. Well, to make a start, you can get rid of your London flat right away. If you should ever need another place, then I'll supply it. And secondly, you can forget about a teaching post, or anything else, at the moment, and about leaving the big house to live here. These sort of decisions are not beyond my intelligence, but don't let my generosity fool you. It's limited. Eventually there are things you'll have to decide for yourself.

'Such as . . .?' she gasped, no proper gratitude assailing her senses, rather a blind flame of anger at his excessive conceit.

His hand caught her as she began to move away while his hard laughter went over her head. 'Such as when you met the right man, my dear Sue. If you don't recognize him yourself, don't come running to me.'

Her grey eyes clouded with impotent fury as she tried to escape his cruel fingers; as she tried to match his laughter but could only manage a flippant remark. 'I don't think I should worry you on that account. I hope I'm quite capable of choosing my own friends.'

'Which isn't exactly the same thing, and I doubt it.' His reply was as audacious as his grip on her waist. She stopped struggling. Against his superior strength she was helpless. Besides, she had a suspicion that he enjoyed taunting her. Probably with the intention of punishing her a little for pestering him with her problems, when he must surely have enough of his own.

His voice came, full of soft derision, in her ear as she stood tensely within his hands. 'I don't think you'd find anything much wrong with your own emotional responses if you gave them a chance. You can't keep them in a refrigerated container for ever.'

Stormily she swung around, her eyes alight with hostility, an attempted defence against her young vulnerability. Illogically she cried, 'How I tick underneath can be of no interest to you. You don't run my life!'

'I'm willing to take anything on – at a price.' Still the gleam of mockery ran through his eyes, but blindly she didn't see it. She only saw the size and bulk of him. The hardness which she coveted but could never achieve.

Colour smouldered recklessly in her cheeks. 'You may be my father's manager, but you can't expect to manage me!'

'Is that so?' His dark head went back with considerable menace as he stared down at her polished skin, the sheen on her fair, heavy hair. 'I'll admit I have known myself to be mistaken about people, but not often.' His mouth moved and she knew he was angry. 'It seems that mere words aren't enough to convince you. There are other ways which you might appreciate better.'

With deliberate intent he moved his hands slowly to her shoulders, in such a way as to stop the breath in her throat. She was conscious of his physical nearness and a trembling assailing her limbs. He was holding her imprisoned between the wall and his body. The kettle boiled and his hand went out to switch off the gas, but he made no attempt to let her go. His eyes had never left her pale face. 'You've succeeded in arousing my curiosity as well as my temper, a rather dangerous combination, would you not agree?'

Sue imagined she felt the impact of his kiss seconds before his lips came down on hers. Desperately she tried to retain the tension in her body, but anticipation clouded her mind as it sharpened her physical response. Strength drained out of her when, as if determined to scatter the last remnants of her resistance, his arms tightened, pressing her softness against him, his eyes stabbing sharply through her as her own closed before the ruthlessness of his.

Against the strength of his arms and his obvious experience she was helpless, yet while instinct warned her not to struggle, her traitorous body wouldn't allow her to remain passive in his arms. Her hands lifted in a feeble attempt to push him away, but only managed to reach his chest where the feel of his hard muscles seemed to shatter coherent thought. With a soft moan she felt sensation explode through her like splintering glass, sending her arms up around his neck, to cling tightly where his hair grew down to a clean smoothness at the back of his head. His lips moved over her mouth, bruising the soft skin, and aroused in her a response which was frightening in its intensity.

At last with narrowed eyes he raised his head, pushing the tumbled hair back from her brow, the better to see her flushed face. It wasn't the hand of a man unused to making love. Sue was quick to realize this, but not to care. It was there, in the thin red line of difference between the boys she had known and a man who knew what he was doing. Her heart beating unevenly kept time with her frantic pulse as she lifted her heavy eyelids and stared at him, stunned. His arms and lips had aroused a mad, dizzy sort of magic, like riding a shooting star, and she suddenly didn't want him to stop.

'Please . . .' she whispered against his mouth.

But he drew back, his dark face intent within inches of her own. 'Does that mean, Miss Frazer, that you would like a repeat performance, or that you want me to let you go?'

His voice had a note of cynicism, so slight that she could have been mistaken. Only his eyes, curiously watchful, told her she was not. Yet his ironic question startled her, bringing her to her senses, stilling a wild confession that she desired only to stay where she was.

With a jerk she pulled away from him. 'Of course I want you to let me go! If it pleased you to kiss me then consider it payment for time spent listening to my foolish conversation.'

His mouth quirked with unexpected amusement. 'Tut-tut, Miss Prunes and Prisms! Not many girls who enjoy my caresses are capable afterwards of such a lengthy speech. I must be slipping!'

'You beast!' It was all she could think of, a feeble reprisal and not at all effective. Meric continued to hold her lightly, to study her indignant face and tremulous parted lips with the uttermost satisfaction. 'Somehow I hardly think you'll question your complete normality again. In spite of your derogatory remarks you might have reason to be grateful to me yet.'

'You're hateful!' Furious colour licked under her skin. She felt like a butterfly on a pin, knowing that her naïveness amused him, that while her immature response might have flattered his ego, it had not impressed him physically. Desperately she struggled to be free, a pulse beating painfully at the base of her throat, and he watched it as he held her, seeming to forget place and time. Then, so suddenly that she almost fell, his arms weren't around her any more. She was free as with a swift movement he turned to the still hot kettle and began pouring water into the mugs.

Once filled, he put them on to a tray with a basin of sugar. 'Open the door for me, there's a good girl. We may as well have this now that it's ready.' His keen eyes flicked to her face and she felt unpredictable tears stinging her eyelids. Quickly she did as he instructed, hurrying into the other room, suddenly afraid that he should notice. The knowledge that he disturbed her she would rather keep to herself.

She went back to her chair by the fire, scarcely aware that

he had put the tray on the table until a smothered exclamation jerked her around. With dismay she saw that his eyes
were fixed on the letter which she had been writing to Tim
before he had arrived. Uneasily she remembered the exact
wording, wishing fervently that she hadn't left it where
Meric could see it. Now it was too late! She saw the scepti-
cism, the touch of derision at his mouth as he picked up the
sheet of notepaper.

'And who is Tim?' he demanded, slanting a glance at her
perturbed face, ominously quiet.

The change in him was barely perceptible, yet it was
there. Never had Sue felt more like running away, or wishing that the ground would open and swallow her up. He
stood there like the day of judgement, scattering her wits
when she most needed them. 'Just a friend,' she managed to
croak at his arrogant eyebrows.

'Just a friend,' he repeated with extreme dryness, scru-
tinizing her closely. 'Why write as if you'd won the
pools?'

'I don't know how you come to that conclusion,' she
faltered. How could she confess, in his present mood, that
she knew very well what he meant? It wasn't what she had
intended putting down, and she had been going to tear it up.

Disparagingly he rapped out, 'I'm afraid you don't fool
me one bit. Not now. A girl who responds as you do in a
man's arms wouldn't be without boy-friends!'

In the half-light his face was grim, and Sue shrank back
suddenly cold. 'It's not what you think,' she gasped, through
stiff lips.

'I'm not gullible, nor am I a fool. What happens next?
You'll be having dear Tim along to view the promised land?
Your rich inheritance?'

'How dare you!' she flung at him, rage replacing her
former dismay, her face white. 'You're quite mistaken in
your horrible assumptions. Tim was kind after the accident,
that's all.'

85

He brushed this aside with a sardonic grin, his eyes sluing over her. 'In your arms, Sue, a man might find it easy to be kind.'

'You're insufferable – and forgetting your place!' Sheer desperation hurtled the words recklessly from Sue's lips, as her chin lifted furiously. 'If you think I enjoyed your kisses then you're mistaken. Against your brute strength I was forced to submit.'

She heard him laugh ambiguously above her head and, as before, she knew that she had aroused him, if without lasting effect. 'I shouldn't like to call you a little liar, Sue. The next time we get together I must see you're better pleased.'

'Sometimes I hate you!' she said clearly.

'A complete waste of emotion.' His gaze rested darkly on her hot face, her bruised mouth, but when he spoke again his voice was level and somehow remote. 'I should advise you to wait and see the size of the estate before completing your missive. I intended asking if you would come with me tomorrow. A sort of conducted tour, if you like.'

'Only if I have no choice?'

'If you can find a suitable explanation. John is especially keen that you should see around. I shouldn't wish to inflict my company on anyone, but we have quite an expanse of rather wild territory which it wouldn't be safe for you to negotiate alone. Besides, you don't know the boundary lines.'

'It's taken you quite a while to get around to it,' she accused sharply, because in a curious way his accusations and indifference hurt. 'At least Tim Mason knew how to treat me like a – like a lady,' she finished, for want of a better word.

'Good for you.' He glanced meaningfully at the note-paper, his voice sarcastic again. 'Obviously in his case it's paid off, but don't you ever get tired of being handled with kid gloves?'

Again Sue's face flamed with her temper as her eyes

locked with his. Did he really intend piling insult on injury? 'I suppose in South Africa you had a different approach, but it might not be one that every girl appreciates.' She longed, with a pent-up resentment, to fling Carlotte at his head along with all her secret suspicions, but suddenly she dared not. Suddenly her anger seemed to evaporate as quickly as it had come, leaving her tired, oddly drained, and she turned away. 'I think it might be better if we both went home,' she added simply, and with as much dignity as she could muster.

He made no response, just shrugged his wide shoulders, his eyes empty of both amusement and anger. Smoothly he folded her letter and passed it to her before bending to switch off the fire and hustle her out of the door. 'The next time you feel like writing to London,' he said, 'write to your solicitor instead of Tim, and ask him to look into that lease on your flat.'

Unavoidably, it seemed, Sue's tour of Glenroden had to be postponed owing to the state of the weather. During the next few days immediately following her quarrel with Meric rain fell incessantly, while mist shrouded the hills. With autumn scarcely arrived, winter would seem to be following too closely behind, but John assured her that there were many fine days yet to come.

'It's all just part of Scotland, I suppose,' he remarked, as they sat in the library one afternoon after tea, watching the rain driving hard against the window. The wind, joining forces, swept through the branches of the old pine forest on the edge of the grounds. Hurtling all before it, it scattered the first fallen leaves untidily across the rough-mown lawns, leaving them lying, fragments of crimson and gold.

'The weather, you mean?' Lazily Sue glanced slowly away from the window, idly contemplating the blazing yellow logs in the fireplace. It had been one of John's good days in spite of the monsoon outside, and they had spent the greater part of it on his book. Today they had almost completed the rough notes on a whole chapter dealing with the history of the old Ruthven barracks, scene of the last act of the Jacobite Rising, where after the Battle of Culloden, rebel clansmen, followers of Charles Edward, had waited, only to receive the heartrending message to disperse. Sue's typing had improved daily, as had her grasp of the whole Rising, which delighted her father, who had confessed that secretly, at one time, he had doubted ever finishing even the first part of his book.

Now, feeling refreshed and rested again, she contemplated going for a walk. 'Not far,' she assured John, as he raised anxious eyebrows towards the streaming window. 'I'll never sleep if I don't get some air. I'll take Bruce,' she ruffled the ears of his dog who lay stretched out at their feet. 'He's getting lazy, like me. A good walk will do him good. Maybe,' she hesitated, avoiding his quiet eyes, 'I could take Meric's dog too? He won't have done much today – the dog, I mean – but sit in the Land-Rover, if he's been out at all.'

'Well . . .' John nodded, only half convinced but conscious of his daughter's pale face. 'Run along, then. Sometimes the weather does ease up after tea. I think you'll find Rex in the study with Meric. Remember he said he was going to sort out some accounts when he looked in before?'

Sue nodded, not waiting a second bidding, jumping quickly to her feet. Belatedly she tried not to appear too eager, but was unable to restrain her dancing feet. She had seen very little of Meric since that night at the cottage and, in spite of what had passed between them, she found herself thinking of him continually. It was surprising, both living in the same house as they did, how little she saw of him. He usually dined out and took sandwiches and a flask for lunch, and usually had eaten his breakfast and gone long before she was up. Sometimes, stupidly, she found herself longing for winter with its dark cosy evenings, when surely he must spend more time indoors.

88

'I'll go now,' she smiled lightly, calling to Bruce. 'If you'll be all right? Mrs. Lennox has gone, but I'll be back in plenty of time to get dinner. Meric will be around if you need anything.'

Humming softly to herself, she collected her waterproof from a cupboard in the kitchen, remembering to stoke up the cooker and replace the hob before she went out. The oven should be nice and hot when she returned. Jamming a matching hat on her fair, fluffy hair, she left the room, running over the wide hall to knock quickly on the study door as she pushed it open.

Startled, and not a little embarrassed, she drew back, her breath catching painfully in her throat. Carlotte was there, in Meric's arms. Sue stopped dead and blinked. True, Meric just held the girl lightly, but he was smiling gently into her face, which was clearly that of a girl who had recently been kissed. His expression, Sue noted indignantly, didn't change as he lifted his head and saw her standing in the doorway. Antagonism surged through her so that it took an almost physical effort to remain there looking at them, to keep a smile fixed on her own face so that neither the two of them should guess the chaotic state of her feelings.

'I'm taking Bruce out,' she stammered uncomfortably, forgetting to greet Carlotte, attempting to explain her own intrusion when no one spoke. 'I thought Rex might like to come with us?' She could see nothing but the inquiring tilt of Meric's eyebrows, the sharp glint of humour in his dark eyes.

It was Carlotte who spoke first, sleek satisfaction glowing over her face as she viewed Sue's discomfiture. 'Don't let me stop you,' she murmured. 'I just popped in to see Meric. The dog's over there.'

The soft insolence in her voice must have been audible only to Sue, as Meric didn't so much as bat an eyelid. With a regretful sigh he released the girl, his mouth quirking wryly. 'Perhaps Miss Frazer guessed I wasn't getting on with my work, my love. She's been at it all day, I believe, on her typewriter. A proper little slavedriver!'

Sue, her cheeks hot, ignored his satirical remarks as she called sharply to Rex, almost grateful that Bruce was impatiently pushing her towards the door. 'I'll see you later,' she retorted coolly, returning his dry smile with a blank stare. 'I must apologize if I interrupted something.' That it seemed impolite to depart so quickly without offering Carlotte even a cup of tea, Sue did not care. She had no wish to subject herself to an hour of Carlotte's sharp tongue. Undoubtedly Meric would supply her with a drink – along with other things! As she hastily closed the door her eyes fell on two half-empty glasses. She need not have worried about a lack of hospitality!

A peculiar rage churned through Sue's heart as she swiftly ran from the house. As if countless demons were chasing her. Yet, as she slowed down on the rough grass track which led to the forest, she was forced to admit she was being slightly ridiculous. That Meric Findlay shared some sort of relationship with Carlotte seemed obvious. But it was equally obvious that it was entirely his own business.

Unhappily Sue tried to collect her senses and keep an eye on the two golden Labradors as they ambled off into the trees. It seemed little use denying, here in the primitive forest, that she was attracted to Meric Findlay herself. Almost in love with him, she supposed wretchedly, refusing to admit the futility of that qualifying adverb. The rain stung her face; the wind tore at her clothing, but she scarcely felt it, as the wildness of the elements found an answering reaction in her own heart. Unleashed in her she felt emotions streaming, and knew a wild, uncivilized urge to rush back and accuse him of philandering. Which seemed even more ridiculous than her previous thoughts, and filled her with dismay. This, she supposed, was jealousy, plain and undiluted!

Impatient with herself, Sue stopped and leaned against a tall fir, striving for some measure of composure, grateful that there was no one to witness her despondency. Meric Findlay had chosen to kiss her as a form of punishment, nothing else. He hadn't liked her alluding to his status as manager. How he could be sensitive about such a small thing, she didn't know. She had been here long enough to realize that Glenroden couldn't be run without him. Her father was really just a figurehead, and she herself could never presume to have any real say in the matter. But, one of these days, she must insist on knowing Meric's exact position, and refuse to be sidetracked by one of John's evasive replies.

If only, she wished, not for the first time, she had known her father from childhood in the normal way. Then she might have found it easy to persist, to expect utter frankness in most things, to find it possible to rely partly on intuition, born from years of association, to be aware of many things without having to ask. It seemed dreadful still to feel so often a stranger, utterly bereft of the warmth and comfort of a deeper relationship. Feeling as she did there was really only one sensible thing to do. If nothing else it would stop her becoming completely obsessed with Glenroden and its occupants. This, she admitted with utter conviction, was the road to disaster. She knew that!

To her surprise Carlotte was waiting in the drive when Sue returned. She had stayed out longer than she had intended, in a vain attempt to get rid of her vibrant unrest. As John had predicted, the rain had eased off, if only slightly, and the walk up through the forest was reasonably sheltered and dry. There had even been a glimpse of sunshine which, as it broke through the heavy layer of cloud, had touched the mountain tops with yellow and pink, making a sparkling tracery through branches of spruce and pine. There was something beautiful in the silence of the forest which she especially loved and as usual was loath to leave. John often talked about the forests, how they teemed with a wild life of their own, but so far Sue had seen little sign of the birds and animals he appeared to know so well. The thing was, she supposed, she didn't know what to look for, or where to find it. Maybe, she thought wistfully, she might find the courage to ask Meric to show her some time.

Damp, but feeling refreshed if not enlightened, she did not particularly welcome the sight of Carlotte sitting in her car, and quickly searched her mind for an excuse not to linger. 'It's later than I thought,' she smiled politely. 'I must hurry or there won't be any dinner!' Then, before she could stop herself, she heard herself saying, possibly because of her earlier lack of hospitality, 'Won't you stay and have a meal with us? It will only be simple, but you're very welcome.'

As usual Carlotte's smile didn't quite reach her eyes. 'Meric is taking me out to dinner in Perth, so I won't need to trouble you. He's picking me up in an hour, so you aren't the only one in a hurry. Right now he's been called out for a few minutes by one of the men.'

Sue's face felt suddenly stiff. So this was what Carlotte had waited to tell her! She might have known that it wasn't just a friendly gesture. 'Don't let me keep you, then,' she retorted with a shrug. 'In any case, Meric seldom dines at home.'

Again satisfaction gleamed furtively in Carlotte's eyes, but apparently her reason for lingering had been two-fold. She startled Sue by ignoring her note of dismissal and saying blandly, 'Meric and I are old friends and often dine together. We have done for years. I'm not quite sure of his exact position with Cousin John, here at Glenroden, but as it's probable that one day I get the lot, I'm not going to quibble over the balance of things.'

Blankly Sue stared at her, knowing intuitively that Carlotte's statement, if one could call it that, was a sort of throwing down the gauntlet. Carlotte obviously felt the time had come to let her know exactly where she stood, along with a subtle warning that it had better not be in her way. But she was also trying to find out if Sue was in possesssion of the true facts concerning the estate, Sue was certain of this.

A small spate of anger rushed through Sue's head. It seemed that Carlotte was prepared to go to any lengths to satisfy her curiosity, to get the information she was after; the information which she insisted was not important. She was quite prepared to use any devious method which she thought might work. Coolly, Sue spoke. 'So far as I know, Carlotte, Meric Findlay is just the manager, so there isn't really any mystery. If it's a wealthy husband you're after, then I'd advise you to look elsewhere.'

There was a sharp silence as Sue stood back, rigidly polite, waiting for Carlotte to go. The car engine roared abruptly into life, calming down slightly as Carlotte impatiently slammed the door and wound down the window, easing her foot from the accelerator. A faint flush stained her cheekbones, otherwise she appeared quite calm.

'A word in your ear, too, Miss – er – Frazer,' she replied. 'I never did like people who get in my way. It might pay you to remember!'

The letter from London which Sue had waited for came next morning, sooner than she had expected. She read it through quickly, and was just finishing her coffee and toast when Meric thrust his head around the door.

'Not bad news, I hope?' His glance took in the letter and her thoughtful face.

Sue lifted her head and looked at him, surprised that he should be around at this time of the morning, her eyes quick to note the fine lines of strain about his firm mouth, a faint weariness in his dark eyes. Undoubtedly he had had a late night! 'Since you ask,' she answered, 'it's from my solicitor, but not really bad news.'

He waited, eyebrows raised, as she hesitated before going

on somewhat reluctantly, 'He doesn't see any difficulty in getting rid of the flat, this sort of accommodation being so much in demand, but he thinks I'll have to return and deal with the furniture and any personal belongings myself. It's not so much the furniture,' she frowned more anxiously than she realized, 'the whole lot put together wouldn't be worth very much – I mean, on today's second-hand value. We don't have any antiques, I'm afraid. But there's my clothing and books, and various other items which no one could sort out but myself.'

'Of course not.' He accepted her rather muddled explanation with a brief, concise nod, then stepped into the kitchen to fill a mug of coffee from the still hot pot. 'As a matter of fact I've had some correspondence from London myself this morning, which necessitates my going there too. It might be a good idea if you travelled down with me, say in a couple of days' time.'

CHAPTER SIX

THE plane from Turnhouse Airport to London seemed to be full of wealthy tourists and business men. Sue subsided quickly into her seat, not because she was glad to sit down – she had been sitting all the way from Glenroden that morning – but because she and Meric were not on their own. Carlotte was with them. They had picked her up at Perth, and now she was sitting in front with Meric, her dark head very near his shoulder.

Irrationally, the only grain of comfort which Sue could glean from the situation lay in the fact that Meric had not been directly responsible for Carlotte being here. It was only yesterday, when Carlotte had called, that John had innocently mentioned Sue's pending trip, adding that Meric was going too. Carlotte, quick-witted as usual, had professed to be delighted. It would be an ideal opportunity to visit her mother who lived in Kent, she said. They could all travel together.

Sue had been surprised to learn that Carlotte had a mother, until she remembered when she had first met her in Edinburgh. Carlotte had been on her way to see her mother then, but it seemed strange that she didn't live with her all the time. She had asked John about it when Carlotte had gone in search of Meric, to arrange to be picked up.

'Her mother married again,' John told her briefly, 'years ago, but for some reason or another Carlotte doesn't get on with her stepfather, so doesn't live with them. She visits, and her mother comes to Edinburgh, but that's as far as it goes. Just as well, really,' he had grunted, 'as Carlotte likes to rule the roost.'

Sue hadn't asked any more questions, content to leave it at that. Carlotte obviously had a legitimate excuse for her journey, she decided, as she fastened her seat belt following the instructions of the charming stewardess. Come to that it might not be fair to call it an excuse at all. Seemingly Carlotte visited her mother quite often. It made sense that she didn't like to travel on her own.

All this sweet reasonableness on Sue's part didn't stop her glancing wistfully in Meric's direction as the plane took off. This was her very first flight, although he didn't know it, and she would have welcomed him by her side. Instead she had a tired-looking tourist, to whom flying was obviously no novelty as she was already half asleep. Rather frightened, as the huge Trident left the ground, Sue closed her eyes, trying to concentrate her thoughts on something else.

It was actually four days since that morning in the kitchen when Meric had suggested this trip. She hadn't been easily persuaded, and even now she was wondering if she'd been wise. Quickly opening her eyes, she stared at the back of his dark head and broad shoulders, still uncertain that she was doing the right thing.

At the time Meric had swept her doubts impatiently to one side. 'It seems the sensible thing to do,' he had pointed out emphatically. 'You might need help of some kind, and your friend Tim Mason might not be available.' This last with a glint in his eye.

Sue had found herself protesting hotly without meaning to. 'I should have to let Tim know . . .'

'Know what?' His question had cut through the sharp morning air.

'That I'm giving up the flat, of course. He's been keeping an eye on it for me.'

'Which means that he has a key?' The glint in his eye had deepened, not very pleasantly.

Sue still remembered the heat in her cheeks as she had flashed him a look. 'It's not what you think! There was no one else.'

'So you keep telling me, Susan my darling, but you must

96

be prepared to admit that it rather strains the credulity?'

The evening before he had called Carlotte 'my love'! Was there no limit to his arrogance!' 'You must think what you will,' Sue had replied stiffly. 'You seem to enjoy putting the worst construction on anything I do.'

He had stared at her closely for a long tense moment before appearing to shake off his black mood with a mocking twist of his lips which might have been a smile. 'Put it down to jealousy if it makes you feel better, Sue. Other women have derived much pleasure in doing just that.'

'Where you're concerned?' Her raised eyebrows had imbued the question with a fine contempt, and for a split second his brilliant dark gaze had hardened threateningly.

Then suddenly his dry smile had deepened into a ring of laughter. He was amused and not troubling to hide it. 'Just when I feel like putting you over my knee, I find myself wanting to do something else! To be on the safe side we'd better get back to our original discussion.'

While her heart had turned over in her breast he had talked casually of flying to London, of going down one day and coming back the next. Only an hour from Edinburgh, he had said, but he didn't mention expense! She had had no idea how much it would be, but surely it was much more expensive than going by car or rail? When she had mentioned this tentatively, he had exclaimed:

'If you're worrying about the cost, then don't! I think Glenroden can take care of that. You haven't been exactly idle over the last few weeks. Consider it in lieu of salary, if it will make you feel better.'

Sue's hands clenched angrily on her lap. How he loved to ride roughshod over people's feelings! His few ambiguous remarks had told her quite clearly that he realized she had little money to spare of her own. She had longed tempestuously to throw his offer back in his face, but something, she knew not what, stopped her, and the moment in which she might have refused came and went, leaving her lips to utter a formal protest, but only weakly, 'How could we both be away when Father's so ill?'

'So ill?' For an instant she had thought Meric looked startled. 'Yes, I suppose he is,' he conceded guardedly. 'But he could go on the way he is for years. His condition isn't critical. In between attacks he keeps fairly well. I think we might safely leave him for a couple of days with Mrs. Lennox. It wouldn't be the first time she's looked after him, and there are plenty of men around the place should she need any help.'

A hundred doubts had continued to plague her mind, in spite of what Meric said, yet the idea of going with him wasn't to be resisted. The true reason for Meric's going might be clouded in obscurity. She had a suspicion, which she tried to discard, that it was to ensure she returned. John, who was obviously relieved that at last she was getting rid of the flat, had possibly asked him to go, and he couldn't refuse. Whatever the reason, she had been in the mood to clutch at straws without querying too closely what had prompted them to blow in her direction.

The plane was comfortable and well heated, for which Sue was grateful. The coat she wore was thin, too thin for October in the Highlands. From the flat she would collect her warmer clothing. At least, if not very up to date, it would see her through until she was in a position to earn some money for replacements. After take-off she found herself enjoying the flight, the thrill of a new experience dissolving some of her previous gloom. The wide vista of the British Isles spread out below them was breathtaking. Viewed from this angle everything looked completely different, and although many landmarks eluded her she found the trip absorbing enough to keep her mind off the two in front.

All too soon, it seemed, they were at Gatwick. Incredibly it was little after three hours since they had left Glenroden, the flight from Edinburgh having taken just over an hour.

With the whole day still in front of her, Sue didn't even feel tired, and within a short time Meric was dropping her off in Kensington outside the flat.

He told the taxi to wait while he escorted her to the door, refusing her invitation to come in, but staying to insert the key for which she fumbled in her bag. 'You'll be all right?' The question could have been a statement, as his eyes swept her paler face.

'Of course!' Inadvertently her glance wavered away from his, going past him to where Carlotte sat impatiently in the taxi. It would be senseless to confess that now she was here, a host of misgivings beset her. While she had been away it had seemed possible to put the tragedy of her mother's death behind her. Now it seemed to be coming back to haunt her, making her curiously reluctant to enter the flat. But how could she explain all this to Meric especially when he was obviously not disposed to linger, and even finding the right words might be impossible.

Besides, she had a sudden feeling he was a stranger. For the first time since she had known him he had abandoned his kilt for a dark blue town suit, in which he still looked extraordinarily attractive, but in an entirely different way. With his change of dress came a bewildering sophistication. That he was a man of the world, and of some experience, was quite apparent. It didn't need the added incentive of well-groomed hair and smoothly shaved skin to confirm it. She could think of nothing to add to her brief observation.

A slight frown creased his dark brows as she stood waiting for him to go. 'Don't forget,' he said, 'that you're staying at the hotel tonight.' Again he named the well known establishment which he had mentioned earlier. 'I'll probably be dining elsewhere, but I'll check before I turn in to see if you've arrived.'

Numbly Sue nodded as she watched him drive off, a smile, which she hoped appeared grateful, fixed to her lips. She had no doubt that he would be spending the evening with Carlotte, although he hadn't actually said so. Neither had Carlotte said anything about hurrying down to Kent! The flatness of unreasonable despair almost overwhelmed Sue as she closed the flat door behind her.

For the next hour she tried desperately to adjust her feelings, but somehow the flat didn't seem like home any more and she felt unable to associate herself with the place where she had spent a greater part of her life. Wandering aimlessly from room to room she couldn't attach to any of it much reality. The brief apprehension she had known when she had first arrived faded quickly, and she felt no familiar stirring of distress. At Glenroden she had imagined the different environment accountable for her swiftly diminishing pain, but it was almost as if the life which she and her mother had led together had never been and, as before, Sue searched for some flaw in her own character which might explain her apparent heartlessness.

In the end she gave up trying to analyse her reactions and set to work. The rooms were small, but on closer inspection, in spite of what she had told Meric, the furniture was comfortable and of excellent quality. All of which, she saw bitterly, reflected the generosity of her father's allowance, if she had but known it. It seemed a shame to let it go with the flat for probably next to nothing. Eventually, after collecting and packing her few personal belongings, she decided to ring Tim and ask if there was anything he would like. Perhaps it would be a nice way of saying thank you for all that he'd done.

She had been going to ring Tim in any case to let him know she was here, only she had forgotten that both the telephone and electricity had been cut off while she was away. It seemed more feasible to wait until nearer lunch time, as now she must go to the kiosk at the end of the street. When she was out she would find a café and have something to eat.

Tim was delighted but surprised to hear from her, and

immediately insisted on taking her to lunch. 'You should have let me know,' he reproached her indignantly. 'I've been waiting daily for all the details of your remarkable adventure, and then you turn up! I've been trying desperately to get extra leave. I might have passed you on my way to Scotland, which wouldn't have been much good!'

Sue stared at him, aware of a flicker of dismay. Tim had brought her to the same restaurant where they had last had a meal together on that August day before she had gone to see her mother's solicitor. When he had asked her to marry him, and she had refused. Or at least – she tried to remember with painful honesty – she had put him off because she hadn't been enthusiastic, which probably wasn't quite the same thing. Strange that she had almost forgotten such a momentous event. At the moment she could only feel disturbed that he had considered following her to Glenroden. 'I don't think it would be a good idea. Not now.'

Tim finished ordering before he replied, and a quick glance told Sue that her words had offended. Without much perception it was possible to read Tim like a book. He said now, his mouth pursed, 'Surely it would be a good idea for me to come and check up? A wealthy father with a weak heart could need careful handling. Someone should be there to look after your interests!'

'I didn't ever say he was wealthy, Tim!' Sue started at the casual mundanity of his remarks. 'That is ... Well, I suppose he is quite well off, but I don't know any details.'

'There you are!' Tim's voice was laced with triumph. 'So easily deceived, my dear Sue. This manager fellow you talk about. In a situation such as you describe, that's the type to watch!'

'But I haven't described anything, Tim. You're making it up. I've only given you the bare facts. My father's ill. I haven't pried.'

'Then you should have done, darling, for your own good. I'm only giving you the benefit of my experience. I'm used to reading between the lines. It's part of my job.'

Tim must be indispensable to his tax office! 'Please,' she tried to stem the self-righteous flow.

He brushed her weak protest aside, his brown eyes sullen, 'You tell me that you're giving up the flat, leaving London for good. What am I to think – or do?'

'Tim,' Sue stared at him unhappily, 'you said when I first went to Scotland that I might find an elderly relation in need of care and attention. Well, my father had this long before I arrived, but I think he does need my companionship, and I intend to stay, just so long as he wants me. It's probably irrelevant that I happen to like Glenroden, but I do. I'm only giving up the flat because it isn't practical to keep it on. It doesn't mean I won't come back one day.'

'But it's highly unlikely. This manager fellow . . .'

'I wish you wouldn't go on about him!' Sue interrupted sharply. 'He does a splendid job. I don't think he has any designs on my father's property, and as a matter of fact, he came down with me today.'

'Good heavens!' Tim pushed away his soup as if his appetite had gone. 'See what I mean? He obviously can't let you out of his sight. Maybe he thinks he'll have you along with the estate when the old man goes.'

'Tim!' This time Sue's voice was cold as she stared at him as if he had struck her. 'You've no right to say such things. If you must think them then kindly keep such thoughts to yourself. I've explained the whole situation. If you can't accept it . . .'

'Oh, hell, I know that!' Tim shrugged elaborately. 'And being a fool I'm deliberately bungling my chances.' Remorsefully he leant across the table to engulf her hand with his, his expression pleading forgiveness. 'It's you I'm thinking about, Sue. You know I've loved you for a long time.'

Which was news to Sue, although she didn't actually say so. True, he had asked her to marry him, but partly she suspected with a view to settling in a comfortable flat. He had made no bones about the fact that he found her home attractive. Also attractive might be a wife with a small income of her own, plus the training and ability to earn a good salary. Besides, wasn't his boss often hinting that the right wife could give a man the kind of stability he needed to put him in line for promotion?

She knew an extra start of dismay when he added smoothly, 'If you're heiress to a Highland estate, any kind of estate for that matter, you need someone to look after your interests. This manager . . .'

'Meric Findlay is not interested in me personally, if that's what you're getting at,' Sue broke in heatedly. Bleakly the truth of her statement paled her hot cheeks. As she stared back at Tim her grey eyes clouded with inner distress, grateful only that he couldn't guess the true state of her feelings.

'And you expect me to believe that?' Speculatively his eyes swept the fine, clear outline of her face, the heavy, swinging hair which seemed to have acquired an extra polish from its weeks of freedom, the sensitive, curved mouth.

Sue bit back an angry answer, not wishing to quarrel with him. It seemed senseless to spend the short time they had together in this way. 'We didn't come down here alone.' The words fell colourlessly from her taut lips. 'There's another girl with us whom Meric likes very much.'

'Oh, I see!' Visibly, a knowing smile on his lips, Tim began to relax, finding nothing to doubt in Sue's forced indifference. 'Well, that's okay, but you know how things are. One can't be too careful, and you never have been very worldly.' He broke off abruptly and looked at his watch. 'The darned time, Sue! I really must go. I'll call for you this evening and we'll have dinner somewhere. It's too bad you didn't let me know you were coming. You put me in quite a spot.'

'Never mind, Tim.' This time she ignored his air of reproach. 'Remember you promised to look over the furniture?'

He nodded, as he struggled into his coat. 'I'd really like to take over your flat completely. It's a lot more comfortable than my place, but according to your lease, subletting is out. Anyway, in my case, as a new tenant, they'd probably bump up the rent out of all proportion, and I couldn't afford it just now.'

Tim's mind ran in circles, Sue grimaced with a wry smile as she watched him depart. It always returned to himself. Still, he was someone she knew and for the first time that she could remember in London she felt lonely. It would have been nice to have spent the afternoon with him. However, there was still plenty to do. Most of the things she wanted to keep were packed. Meric would arrange for these to go by rail, but there were some bits and pieces, old books and such-like which nobody would want. She must ask someone to dispose of those. Maybe the old man with the junk shop in Queen Street would help?

The man said he would, and could call in an hour. Thankful, Sue started back to the flat. It was imperative she should have everything finished so that she could hand over the key to the solicitor tomorrow. In a way, especially if Tim didn't want much, the sale from the furniture might cover the solicitor's fees.

Then at a small boutique on a corner she was sidetracked. It was the display in the large plate-glass window which stopped her so suddenly. Cleverly arranged over a raised pedestal was a chiffon nightgown with a matching negligée in a wonderful rose pink. Entranced, Sue gazed. She could imagine it toning beautifully with her fair hair and grey eyes. Apart from one thin nylon nightie which she had worn during the summer, all her night attire had consisted of pyjamas, usually boys' pyjamas which her mother used to pick up cheaply at sales, which she had always insisted were better value than anything else. Not that Sue hadn't been quite happy to wear them, but this in the window was something special. Not bridal exactly, but very, very nice.

Inside the shop she asked the price and was startled when the woman told her.

'It is really beautiful, madame.' The woman eagerly took the set from the window, to show Sue the intricate filigree of delicate silver on the waist. 'It was just made for a girl like you.' Her eyes flickered admiringly over Sue's slim figure.

Greatly against her better judgment, but with the filmy material between her fingers and unable to resist, Sue agreed to buy. By swift mental calculation she decided she could just about afford it and have enough left over for a warm anorak and pair of slacks. Her money, she knew, was rapidly running out. There hadn't been as much in her mother's account as she had expected, and she had earned nothing herself since going to Glenroden. The sale of her Mini might be one possible way of raising funds, but without it she would lose her independence. There was no bus service within miles of Glenroden, and if she did find a job, which she must, she would inevitably need transport.

But until she did find work such extravagances as this would have to stop. Hastily she took the carefully wrapped parcel from the pleasant, smiling woman, and left the shop quickly before she was tempted to buy more. How practical such a flimsy garment would be in a Scottish winter, she had no means of knowing, yet, in a moment of temporary light-heartedness, she didn't really care.

Long before Tim called for her that evening Sue was tired. She took him back to the hotel, leaving him with a drink while she bathed and changed. And when he suggested that they ate in the hotel's very good restaurant she was more than willing to agree. It was only afterwards, when he talked of going on somewhere, that she demurred, but seeing his disappointed face she gave in. After all, it could be a long time before she was back in London.

It was after midnight before they returned, later than Sue had intended, but the night-club had been fun and, in a strange way, had seemed to release some of the tensions of the past weeks, possibly because of its very gay atmosphere. They had drunk a sparkling white wine and relaxed, talking desultorily. Tim had surprised her by reverting almost to his old companionable self, and when they had said good-bye outside the hotel Sue liked him better than she had done all day. In the morning he and his immediate superior were on their way to Devon to do an important tax assessment, so she wouldn't see him again before she left.

'You mustn't forget to give me a ring and write,' he instructed as he left her. 'If you don't I'll be worrying as usual.'

With what amounted to nearly a sigh of relief, Sue collected her key from the desk and went up to her room. She had half expected that Tim might be awkward. That he might try to extract promises of marriage or meetings, but apart from the few words as he left her, he hadn't said a thing. Perhaps he had decided that if he was patient she would return to London in the near future. He might have been surprised to learn that almost before she closed her bedroom door Sue had forgotten about him.

Once in her bedroom weariness claimed her, washing everything from her mind but the desire to sleep, making even the effort of getting ready for bed insurmountable. In the adjoining bathroom she creamed her face before taking a quick shower. The warm water revived her a little, and she put on her new negligée. In the centrally heated room it would be much more comfortable than the pyjamas still packed in her overnight case.

Ready at last, she climbed into bed, but no sooner was her head on the pillow than there came a knock on the door. Uneasily her heart thudded. Surely Tim hadn't returned? But he wouldn't know her room number, and if she had forgotten something he could have left it at reception. Unhappily as the knock came again she got up, not bothering to switch on the light as she stumbled to the door.

Wrenching it open, she was startled to find Meric standing outside on the corridor. Surprise ran through her, widening her eyes. Determinedly throughout the day she had kept him from her thoughts. Even when Tim had referred to him so disrespectfully she had refused to allow herself to dwell on him for a moment longer than it had taken to defend him fairly. Meric had said, she remembered, he would check to ensure that she was in. Unfortunately she had forgotten all about it. If she had thought about it she might well have pictured him retired for the night, or still out with Carlotte.

'If you wait,' she said blankly, before he could speak, 'I'll put on the light and my dressing gown.'

'Whichever way you like,' he replied sardonically. 'When I think of the time, not to mention the shoe leather, I've wasted traversing between this floor and the two above, another few minutes can't hurt me.' He leaned against the door jamb, casual and relaxed, but his voice was edged with sarcasm.

Sue took one look at him and fled, her fingers fumbling for the light switch as she snatched her wrap from the bed. The bedside lamp lit the room dimly but enough. Conscious suddenly of the thinness of the pink negligée, she hugged her arms around herself as she went back to the door. Meric was already stepping through it.

'Just to make sure you don't start combing your hair and all the other things women tend to do when confronted by a man,' he muttered dryly. 'Even one they don't like.'

As on another occasion she decided he had a fine conceit of himself and her eyes flashed. 'I've done no more than necessary,' she retorted, 'as you can see.'

His eyes went over her tumbled hair, her slightly dishevelled appearance. 'What I see I like,' he grinned. 'It's made my wait rewarding.'

Her eyes, dark smudges of weariness, stared at him apprehensively, missing the smooth satire of his remark. While she didn't appreciate his humour, she could guess that his patience was wearing thin. 'You've been here before?' she asked, rubbing confused fingers across her brow.

'Don't tell me you forgot?' His hard mouth set in lines of mockery and amusement.

'You said you'd check if I was in!'

'And I've been doing just that for the past hour.' His voice jolted her wide awake. 'I thought you'd have the sense to be in before this.' The fathomless eyes flicked over her face, harshly interrogating.

Sue continued to stare at him, her fringed eyes defensive. She need not have worried about being decently covered up. In his present mood he probably wouldn't have noticed had she been naked! 'I spent the evening with Tim Mason,' she said faintly.

'Now I just thought you might.' His voice was a long, cool drawl. 'It also crossed my mind that you must have other friends, but undoubtedly it didn't occur to you to let everyone know you were in town?'

Dazed, as her mind attempted to absorb and dissect, she blinked at him, her pupils dilated. 'It would scarcely have been feasible,' she whispered, her throat constricted. 'I wasn't exactly holding a party.'

With a shrug he moved slightly away from her, his height casting bulky shadows against the wall. Too late she wished she had used the main switch. The light from the small lamp, which flooded palely, was too intimate. She watched nervously as he turned smoothly to face her again. She lifted her head, braced for the onslaught, and he gave a short laugh.

'So you concentrated on one man – Tim from the tax office! And what does he think of your next move? Does he approve, I wonder?'

There was a cleft in Meric Findlay's chin, etched deeply

below his firm, chiselled lips. Sue fixed her gaze on it, refusing to meet the mockery in the dark smouldering depth of his eyes.

She drew a long, quivering breath, and tried to retaliate with a mock flippancy she was far from feeling. 'I could have a tax problem, for all you know. Tim is very obliging. Secondly, he doesn't like the idea of my moving away, but he hasn't actually said much against it. Does that answer your questions?'

'Not completely, but then having no personal knowledge of your friend I don't know how his mind works.'

Sue's shoulders moved just perceptibly. If, as Meric claimed, he didn't know Tim personally, then how did he know he worked for the Inland Revenue? But she wondered idly, too tired to probe, realizing she might only get an evasive reply. A man like Meric Findlay would make it his business to know of anything that could touch him even indirectly. Her presence at Glenroden, if only temporary, no doubt provided an excuse for detailed surveillance.

She mumbled carelessly, scarcely looking at him, 'If I have omitted any relevant information then I'm sure you can supply the deficiency.'

Just as carelessly his hands came down on her shoulders, a means of emphasizing his point, nothing else. 'You'd better decide once and for all that the Tim Masons of this world don't count. Not so far as you're concerned. You can leave him behind tomorrow and start a new life. A clean break is the only way.'

At the touch of his hands an awful feeling of weakness swept over her and she stirred restively, attempting to concentrate on what he was saying, thrusting the merely physical from her mind. Glenroden was important to Meric. It seemed he would go to any lengths to protect it. He nursed the estate along like a baby. No adverse breath of wind was allowed to blow over it! But in doing so, didn't he realize he could be downright hurtful?

'You can't rule everything according to the book,' she cried, fire slipping through her, holding her taut within his hands. 'You should allow for the human element.'

'Your own?' he asked sharply, catching her off guard.

She jerked away from him a little wildly, but he held her still. He looked so strong and unassailable, a man with power to make her feel soft and vulnerable, ready to collapse into his arms.

'Tim and I like each other.' She spoke on a little note of desperation, hugging her body still tighter with her arms. 'I couldn't hope to be as ruthless as you are.'

His wary eyes mocked her. 'You don't strike me as a girl who's been swept off her feet, but perhaps you feel happier with both feet on the ground?'

Aroused, Sue's glance clashed angrily with his. 'The emotional side of my life is none of your business, Meric Findlay!'

'Do you really believe that?' His dark eyes suddenly narrowed, raking her pale skin, her pink negligée, the curtain of ashen hair about her upraised face. 'I remember an occasion when you seemed to enjoy being emotional in my arms. Do you always say please after Tim kisses you?'

A sparkling tension united them, making static the air between them, and her breath escaped audibly through her parted, rose-tinted lips. Irresistibly her eyes were drawn to his mouth, against her better sense. Only too well did she remember the imprint of it on her own from another evening, and longed crazily to repeat the experience. That he should guess the longing which threatened to consume her was utterly beyond comprehension.

'I think I'd like to go to bed,' she said indistinctly, her wits departing with her precarious poise.

His head went back at that, a brilliant smile lighting his dark face as his gaze slid again over her sensual young figure, over the lovely curves of her body which her protective arms revealed, had she but known it, more than they concealed. 'Could that be an invitation?'

His fingers were burning her shoulders through the flimsy material of her gown, and heat swept through her blood like a fever, like nothing she had ever known before, and she quivered with the shock of revelation. Unable to check her trembling, she sought refuge in words. 'Why do you enjoy twisting everything I say? I don't know why you came here tonight, but I do know it's not because you feel attracted to me!'

'You're very charming, Miss Frazer. I shouldn't underestimate your charms if I were you, nor your capacity to enjoy the purely physical in life. Don't tell me that Tim didn't kiss you good night?'

Tim had tried, but she hadn't felt in the mood. At least she had told herself this as she had pushed him away, pleading tiredness. Not that she intended confessing this to Meric Findlay! Resentful that he should even ask, she stayed mutinously silent, until his hands moving over her arms brought sensations which swept everything else from her mind.

Like quicksilver he read the thoughts she tried to hide. 'So you feel cheated. Maybe you would like me to supply the deficiency.' His slanting dark eyes touched the pulse in her throat. He bent his head, slowly and deliberately, and she felt his lips against the bare skin of her shoulder, lingering and drifting over the bone to the nape of her neck, while his fingers curved, pressing soft flesh until she cried out. As a grand finale, as if to punish her a little for even one small note of protest, his head lifted and on her parted lips he dropped a kiss, brief and hard, hurting her in the split second before he let her go.

'Which might just about prove my point,' he spoke tautly. 'That you're not the frozen little iceberg you pretend to be.'

He moved away as she collapsed on to the edge of the bed, barely knowing what she was doing. Nothing of what he alleged could be true, but even if there had been some modicum of truth surely he had no right to inflict his views in this manner?

Her flushed face paled as she stared at him, and her heart turned over. Big and powerful, he stepped back and through her blood ran a wild, stormy longing. Desperately she tried to gather every grain of common sense which had been scattered in those few mad moments in his arms.

In her ear she heard him saying, 'If you'd had the sense to get back in decent time none of this might have happened.'

'So it's my fault?' Childishly she refused to look at him.

'Listen, Sue, I don't intend entering any sixth form argument as to where the blame lies. Maybe,' a faint smile quirked his mouth at one corner, 'it could be placed with the assistant who sold you that very fetching night attire, if that would ease your mind.'

'You surely don't think I bought it specially?' Driven beyond normal constraint, Sue choked untruthfully. 'I've washed it several times.'

'Liar.' His voice was soft, his face full of glinting amusement as he stepped suddenly to her side. 'Unless we now have washable price tags!' Swiftly his fingers pounced, filching a tiny slip of cardboard from the frills on her neckline to show it to her.

Meric's voice was light, purposely mocking, but Sue had lost hers, owing to the hard constriction in her throat. But he gave her no opportunity to answer, dismissing the incident with a brief shrug before he went on, 'It was necessary to see you tonight, Sue, because I have to meet someone again in the morning. I'll probably just manage to catch the afternoon plane by inches. I've settled everything up here and arranged for you to have a taxi to the airport, but I had no idea how you were getting on. For all I knew you could be having difficulties. I had to make sure you were all right.'

He had moved to the door, watching her carefully, his

hand turning the knob as he waited. Sue's gaze, in spite of her attempt to divert it, went tenaciously to his face. Silently she prayed feverishly he would leave quickly, ignoring the intensity of her feelings which cried out just as wildly for him to stay.

She made a tremendous effort to pull herself together, to concentrate on what he was saying as she nodded her head. 'I have an appointment with my mother's solicitor in the morning. I believe there are a few papers to sign, but apart from that I don't think there'll be anything much. I have the key to the flat ready to give him, and he'll see to everything else. I have all my personal belongings packed, like you said ...' Her voice trailed off uncertainly. There didn't seem to be anything more to add.

'Fine, then, I'll see you tomorrow. Go to the airport and wait for me there.' His tone had reverted to normal, alert and decisive. 'I'm sorry it's all been such a rush. Maybe another time we'll have more time to spare.'

Sue flinched as he was gone sharply, and for fully a minute she remained staring at the closed door. If she had been dreaming then her awakening had been too abrupt, almost more than she could cope with. Her hair spilled over her flushed cheeks as despair and taut nerves jerked her into action. Quickly she jumped to her feet, finding her overnight case, tipping the contents haphazardly on to the floor. In a few fumbling seconds she had removed her new negligée, pushing it carelessly to one side before finding her old pyjamas and putting them on. They were a bit short and too boyish, the thin cotton entirely without charm, but in them Sue felt her old, level-headed self.

Satisfied, yet curiously unhappy, she slid back into bed. It might seem a wicked waste of money, but in the morning the pink negligée could go into the dustbin! Or, on second thoughts, she could give it to the little chambermaid with the nice smile. Wherever it went, she never wanted to see it again. If Sue was sure of nothing else, she was sure of that!

CHAPTER SEVEN

ONCE back in Edinburgh Sue tried to view the whole incident sensibly, as merely a trick of the night playing on senses too finely balanced. Meric Findlay was patently not the kind of man to indulge in such interludes, but, she supposed, any man might have his moments of indiscretion. He had probably been as tired as herself, and what had happened had been without design or intent. A clear case of one thing leading to another. Such reasoning, while mundane, was momentarily comforting, and she clung to it as a drowning man might cling to a straw.

They arrived at Turnhouse in the late afternoon, and Meric insisted they had tea before leaving for Glenroden. 'It's a fairish drive,' he said, 'and once on the road I'd rather not stop.'

Sue glanced at him quickly as they drove into the city but made no comment. She had enjoyed the flight better this time. There had been no Carlotte, and Meric had sat with her naming the various landmarks which had eluded her previously. With the expertise of a seasoned traveller he had answered all her questions, telling her all she wanted to know. Unfortunately there had also been time to sit and think, something she hadn't appreciated quite so much.

While she had seen little of Meric in London, in retrospect his rigorous supervision of her affairs was obvious. His tight schedule, his insistence that every aspect of her life in Kensington be neatly packaged, tied up and disposed of in as short as possible time, had been achieved almost it might seem by remote control. Never once had it occurred to her to quarrel with his authority, or to question the fact that he allowed her little leeway of her own. Having always guarded her independence, Sue knew a moment of disquiet, a sneaking premonition that unless she was careful there could be worse to come.

Yet, in spite of an uneasy apprehension, she sighed, murmuring impulsively, 'It's good to be home. Scotland is all I ever dreamed it would be. In two days I've missed it.'

His head half-turned. 'Dreams,' he declared, 'can be dangerous things.'

Hadn't things worked out as he'd planned in London – in his life? 'Do you resent me coming back with you like this?' she asked.

One eyebrow rose. 'Why should I? You have every right,' he declared. 'And your father needs you.'

'But you don't,' she felt like adding, only it would seem an odd question for her to ask. Her mind wandered unhappily to the occasions he had made love to her, then on tenaciously to his friendship with Carlotte. Was it possible he was just playing with them both until he found out who was to inherit Glenroden? Did he hope to be able to choose? John could live for years, but then again he might not. Frightened by her own thoughts, Sue tried not to look into the future. If she had never loved her mother very deeply she still missed her, and in finding her father it seemed she might just as suddenly lose him too. What was the use of loving people if they could be snatched away without warning to leave only an aching void? Even beginning to care for Meric Findlay could only be inviting heartache.

Swiftly as they went down Princes Street she glanced at him, the knowledge of her own foolishness bringing her sharply upright. She was letting a too vivid imagination play tricks! Her eyes turned impatiently to gaze at the fine shops, the cosmopolitan crowds thronging the pavements. Why should she allow a few kisses, the crazy reactions of her impressionable heart, to cause her such torment? Meric must look elsewhere for amusement, and she herself must learn to acquire a thicker skin than the one she had now.

'The capital has a highly dramatic appearance, don't you

think?' Meric glanced at her lightly as they left the car, apparently not at all disturbed by her sudden silence.

Sue nodded as she looked up and her eager gaze fell on the silhouette of the thousand-year-old Castle on its rock and the Old Town stretched against the windy October sky. Across the gardens of Princes Street it was an eye-catching sight.

'The next time we can spare you for a couple of days, you can spend them here and have a good look around.' With a slight smile Meric guided her through the slow moving traffic towards a hotel, his hand firm beneath her elbow. 'It seems a shame we can't stay longer this afternoon, but I'm afraid we'd better push on.'

The drive home was accomplished in record time, or so it seemed to Sue, as she remembered her first lone journey in August. For the main part Meric appeared preoccupied and she found herself dozing off at regular intervals, her tired body subduing her restless mind. It wasn't until they were nearly there that she roused herself sufficiently to ask when Carlotte would be returning. She had tried to ask on the plane, but it was only now, by great effort, she found herself able to phrase the necessary sentence. 'Father enjoys her visits, I think,' she tacked on carefully.

He answered shortly, leaving her strangely unsatisfied, 'She didn't say, and I'm afraid I forgot to ask. No doubt you'll be able to survive without her for a few days.'

She said, 'You don't need to be sarcastic. I just thought you would think it funny that I hadn't asked!'

He replied quietly, 'Forget it. It didn't cross my mind. Usually she doesn't stay away for any length of time.'

His broad shoulders lifted with seeming indifference as he glanced at her sideways. They were silent, aware of each other, but neither willing to say anything more. Sue turned her head away, deploring the tension between them, yet unable to understand it. Her eyes turned towards the moors, looking out through the window to where they lay drenched and bleak from the recent rains. The solitude seemed to reach out and touch her, bringing comfort in the gathering darkness. It was of little use denying that Meric Findlay didn't want her, nor did Carlotte Craig. But Glenroden was fast becoming home to her and no matter what the opposition she intended to stay.

Now that the days were getting shorter, Mrs. Lennox decided she would live in until spring. Doctor McRoberts was still uneasy about John, who seemed to grow frailer each day, and Sue was daily more grateful that the woman was prepared to help look after him. During winter the road between Glenroden and the village was often impassable when the river was in flood and, as Mrs. Lennox pointed out, she could be marooned in the village for days.

Before she could come, however, she had various things to see to, and Sue co-operated by doing more around the house as well as continuing to help John with his book.

'Sometimes, dear, I wonder who's writing it, you or him,' Mrs. Lennox smiled. 'I don't think he would ever have managed it without you.'

'It keeps my mind occupied, and off other things,' Sue returned the friendly smile enigmatically. In spite of Mrs. Lennox's inquiring look she didn't explain that 'other things' mosly constituted Meric Findlay.

Clearly, for all her secret opinion that he was a ruthless adventurer, intent on furthering his own interests, Meric continued to plague her heart. As well as contempt he aroused other emotions which she would rather be without. Whenever she saw him she remembered guiltily that in London she had been on the point of asking her solicitor if he could be properly investigated without arousing suspicion. Yet somehow she had found herself unable to parade all her doubts and fears before the detached legal mind of the law. In the solicitor's office it had suddenly seemed impertinent even to think of broaching the subject, but once back at Glenroden she reproached herself for being a fool.

The opportunity might not come again. If only she had had some idea what such a procedure would involve! Cowardly, she had shrunk from the consequences of wrongly placed judgment. The chance that Meric might be quite innocent of all she suspected, apart from a more or less normal inclination to feather one's own nest. And if she were to mortally offend him without reasonable justification he might leave. Which, she told herself unhappily, would only leave her father in dire straits, and do no one any good.

Time passed. Meric still took out shooting parties, but with the end of October in sight the caravan park was to close for the season. Or so Carlotte said when she returned from London.

'Next year,' Carlotte said smoothly, 'we intend to develop another few acres beside the loch. Subject to planning permission, of course. And, if we get it, I might even be prepared to spend most of the summer here at Glenroden. Meric seems to think I'm indispensable. You probably won't be here, but I thought you might like to know.'

Sue could have retorted that she would rather not have known, that she found the information curiously unpalatable. But there was no denying that, whatever happened, she might not be here. So she remained silent, listening politely as Carlotte chattered on, trying to give the impression that she was completely indifferent as to what happened next year or any time in this part of the world.

According to Carlotte, Meric was taking her out again to dinner, and it added to Sue's increasing bitterness that he had never once asked her. In fact, if anything, he seemed to make a point of keeping out of her way. When, on departing, Carlotte mentioned that she thought a young teacher would be needed in a small school near where she lived, after Christmas, Sue jumped at the idea.

'Let me know as soon as you hear anything definite,' she said, as she waved Carlotte good-bye.

One day towards the end of the month, Meric actually

took her around the estate. He surprised her one evening by asking if she would go, and Sue, disregarding her half-formed intention to refuse, accepted with alacrity.

She was ready soon after breakfast on a fine, if windy October morning. Meric had told her to dress warmly, without regard for fashion as the going would be rough, and the weather unpredictable.

'Don't come dressed in a skirt and thin blouse,' he had said. 'Or I'll send you back to put on something different.'

His slightly threatening tone had been enough to send Sue searching through her wardrobe for a pair of thick slacks, and a heavy sweater which she wore on top of her shirt. She hoped he would consider these suitable.

Mrs. Lennox had also contributed her share towards making their day a success by packing a light rucksack with sandwiches and flasks which she gave to Sue as she came downstairs. 'Enjoy yourself,' she said kindly.

Sue smiled as she ran out to where Meric was waiting. He had the Range-Rover at the door and as she climbed in beside him he released the brake impatiently and they were away. Even now Sue could scarcely believe it.

He glanced at her sideways as they went down the drive. 'You're looking very bright this morning,' he grinned, his impatience forgotten.

She flushed, her smile deepening to laughter as she felt his eyes slide over her miscellaneous attire, right down to her thick stockings and nailed boots. 'You can't complain that I haven't followed your instructions to the letter. I'm prepared for anything, to quote your exact words.'

'Hum ... well,' his eyes still lingered speculatively, 'maybe that wasn't altogether what I had in mind, but as we're going stalking lighter clothing wouldn't do.'

'Stalking?' She stared, her gaze jerking away from the scenery to his dark face. 'You mean – really stalking, after stags and deers?'

He laughed again at that, his eyes glinting as momentarily

they met her own. 'Deer is the plural, nitwit, as you should know.'

'Clever Dick!' she laughed back, greatly daring. 'We had a name for such as you at school.'

'I've known women call me nicer names than that,' he taunted with matching humour. 'My name happens to be Meric. One or twice I've heard you use it yourself.'

Sue's gaze fled back to the distant mountains. She took a deep breath. 'You're very nice when you're friendly,' she said primly, 'but there are times when only Mr. Findlay will do.'

His mouth quirked at the faint note of indignation. He remarked with a touch of mischief, 'Well, for my sins, it's nice to know I arouse positive reactions on occasion. Would you not be prepared to agree with me, sweet Sue?'

She would ... but wild horses couldn't have dragged from her so much as a nod. Nor a plea that he wouldn't refer to her as sweet Sue when he didn't mean it. Instead, she suggested tartly, 'Suppose we stick to the deer?'

'Oh, yes, the deer.' His smile mocked. 'Women are past masters of evasion – if that makes sense. One thing you might learn one day, Sue. You can't run for ever. But for the moment, as you say, we'll stick to the deer.'

'Well?' Her colour heightened, her rather tense query prompted by a sudden jerking of her heart.

He replied smoothly as he swung the large vehicle out on to the major road, 'I hope to show you a stag, several perhaps, and you might see some hinds.'

Intrigued, Sue forgot to be defensive, and turned to him eagerly, her face alight. 'Will we see them on Glenroden? I mean,' she went on cautiously, 'right now I don't know much about Glenroden. Is it a large property?'

Nervously she clutched the edge of her seat, her hands slightly damp with apprehension, hating to admit how little she knew, yet willing to subdue her pride if only to find out more about a place she was beginning to love.

Meric, however, didn't seem at all surprised by what she asked. 'Yes, to both questions,' he said. 'Glenroden is big by some standards, but don't confuse size with profitability. We have a deer forest, some grouse moors, a loch which you've seen. Then lower down we have pine woods, lower hills with sheep, and a few rather poor fields of cereals and root crops. These last fields are improving with care, but the ground remains very stony.'

She found herself frowning, not wholly convinced. There seemed an awful lot of it. 'You say it isn't profitable. Why not? Surely, considering the size, it ought to be?'

For once he must have thought her curiosity pertinent as he appeared quite willing to explain. 'You don't make an awful lot of money on this sort of property. If you own a deer forest you must look after it properly, but it costs quite a lot of money and doesn't pay. Ours does now, now that we have an agreement with the hotel. Some owners let theirs for a season, but you never know what people will do. Sometimes it's all right, but it can be a disaster. This way, the way we do it, the head keeper and myself supervise everything.'

'You mean you let people kill the deer?'

'This way we cull them.'

'By shooting them? That sounds cruel.' As soon as she spoke she knew Carlotte wouldn't have made such a remark.

Meric said, smiling faintly, 'A certain number must be killed every year to prevent the herd increasing.'

Which didn't make sense. Not to Sue, to whom a deer forest was about as familiar as the wilds of Siberia. She considered the information doubtfully. About them there lay plenty of territory, high ground, low ground, miles and miles of it, stretching as far as the eye could see, and not a creature in sight. Surely enough space for hundreds of deer.

'Why can't you let the herd increase?' she asked, bewildered, shifting a little on her seat.

'Because,' he explained quietly, 'there's only a limited food supply. Our deer forest is high and wild. This means that the herd must be kept down to certain numbers, otherwise the beasts would starve before the grass begins to grow in the spring.'

'I see . . .' Considering the bareness of the higher slopes, this seemed logical. Far more logical than the fact that she had been here several weeks and knew so little. Certainly she had never stopped to wonder what all these wild creatures lived on.

They had reached the river by this time, where it ran over the road on its way to the loch. Once across the ford Meric turned right, up a hard but narrow track, running against the river but alongside it, following its rocky bed up through a wood of birch trees, clinging tightly to its twisting path. 'Hang on!' he shouted, as the Range-Rover lurched through a bad dip, throwing Sue against him, hard against his shoulder.

He grinned, and threw an arm around her, steadying her briefly until she regained her balance, after which he needed two hands to control the spinning wheels.

Sue jerked upright and away from him, shrinking into her corner, to obliterate the feel of his hard muscles, the steely grip of his arm. Rather than think about it she hustled her thoughts back to the deer. 'Can't you feed them artificially,' she asked, 'like farmers feed cattle?'

He didn't answer immediately, not until the line of his jaw relaxed to its usual sardonic angle, and his eyes recovered their indifferent dryness. 'Suppose you start at the beginning,' he said, as the track smoothed out and his grip on the wheel eased slightly. 'A deer forest looks enormous on a map, but there are only certain places where there's food, so you can only support a certain number of deer. We know the exact number of deer, that is stags and hinds, which can live comfortably here.'

'So you don't need to feed them?'

'Oh yes. We feed rock salt, beans and potatoes, early in the morning. But it's only in a very hard winter that we might do this. It costs money, and we couldn't do it every year if we didn't have some sort of recompense. Usually the deer forage very well for themselves.'

'You say usually?' Sue's voice quickened with interest.

He nodded, his eyes warmer on her eager face. 'It's the long, hard winter which causes the trouble. The winter when snow lies deep in the corries. Corries, if you don't know, are places where the grass grows, the places where the stags find their food. If the snow lies deep it takes a long time to melt. This is the dangerous time. Once, in such a year, John and I found deer dying of starvation, so weak they couldn't run away, too weak to move when eagles attacked them.'

Sue's breath caught. 'What did you do?'

'Do? We had to shoot them. Put them out of their misery.'

Tightly she closed her eyes, refusing to allow even mental vision. 'Poor things . . . Why don't you always feed them?'

'Well, as I said, or rather implied, it would be too expensive. And if you fed them all the time they would become tame, and there'd be no stalking, and then the forest would get overcrowded.'

'Would that be a bad thing?' Sue's frown returned. 'What would happen if it did?'

'Well, use your imagination, girl. It stands to reason. The deer would come down from the hills, eat the farmers' crops, and the farmers would shoot them. So you see we must cull them. They must be shot by people who know what they're doing. A clean shot is an easy death compared with starvation or bad wounds from a shotgun instead of a rifle.'

The tone of Meric's voice hinted that his patience was not unlimited, but his eyes were still kind, giving her courage to say tritely, 'I shouldn't like to shoot a stag myself, even supposing I knew how to go about it.'

'Fair enough,' his eyes mocked slightly her nervous tremor, 'but you can get quite a lot of fun out of stalking, without shooting or knowing a great deal about it.'

Sue sighed, lapsing momentarily into silence, watching the sun rise higher above the mountains, its beams creeping down the hillside into the valley. It was going to be a fine day. She turned her head to look at him in the closeness of the car. 'You say that any novice can enjoy this sort of thing?' Her hand flicked towards the wildness about them.

'You're twisting my words, Sue.' He returned her curious glance in full measure. 'You shouldn't go wandering around here on your own, if that's what you mean. You must be with someone experienced who knows what they're doing.'

'Is that a warning?'

'It could be . . .' His lips twitched. 'I suspect you could be recklessly headstrong beneath that civilized veneer of yours, but just let me tell you this! If I ever catch you up here on your own, I'll wallop you so hard you won't sit down for a week.'

And he would, too! Colour came surging, tinting her pale skin, but it wasn't anger which flared between them. The thought of such punishment brought a strange excitement where it should have aroused fury. There was something in their relationship which she wouldn't understand. Again she moved away from him. He tended to talk nonsense. She wasn't as he suspected. Right through she was sensible – Tim always said so. Very rarely did she ever act without thinking. She said primly, refusing to give him the satisfaction of knowing he had so much as ruffled her feelings,

'I don't know why you should feel it necessary to issue such a drastic ultimatum, nor what grounds you have for jumping to such outlandish conclusions regarding my character!'

'Just bear it in mind. You might not appreciate it, but a few well chosen words never came amiss. They could even save your life.'

'I think you exaggerate.' Deliberately, as a form of self-defence, she forced a cool note of haughtiness, just to put him in his place. 'I expect your patience can be too sorely tried by our clients at the hotel. But after all, that's your job.'

Instantly his eyes smouldered as with the tilt of her chin his mood swung dangerously, and instantly Sue knew she shouldn't have spoken in this way. It wasn't the first time she had set out to goad him deliberately by implying that he should realize she was the rightful heir to an estate which he obviously coveted. But today he was putting himself out to see that she enjoyed herself and, if nothing else, she should learn to control her tongue and not antagonize him by way of repayment. John, she felt, would not have approved.

But before she could speak his left hand moved with lightning speed, his fingers taking hold of a thick handful of hair at her nape, jerking her neck painfully, and with each small struggle tightening his grip. 'Another word of warning,' he uttered softly as she cried out in pain, not attempting to relax his hold. 'Look about you, Miss – er – Frazer. Look at the wilderness and take care not to try my temper too far. It's supposed to be quite something when properly aroused – ask my men. So take heed.'

He growled in her burning ear before thrusting her roughly away, and she crouched beside him shaking, her eyes fixed mutinously on the track ahead. Fervently she wished she could fade out of sight, or be endowed mysteriously with larger proportions. Then she wouldn't feel so dwarfed and defenceless against his big, powerful body.

He didn't look at her, and she turned quickly from him so that he wouldn't see how she tried to steady herself by gripping her hands tightly together. His rough treatment must have taken her wits away as a clever retort eluded her and she could think of nothing to say. The minutes ticked by silently while her chastised mind restored itself with youthful resilience.

The country on either side was getting wilder, and the track they were travelling seemed barely discernible in the heather. Obviously Meric knew where he was going, but they seemed to have come many miles from Glenroden. Perhaps their slow speed gave this impression? Masking her new nervousness with an air of composure, she asked coolly, 'How much further do we have to go?'

As if aware of her uncertainty and still wishing to punish her a little, he answered smoothly, 'Not much further, but I hope you've recovered sufficiently to walk. If not I'm not prepared to carry you, even supposing you make it an order.'

She looked at her fingers, so that he could only see the sheen of her downbent head. 'I rather asked for that, didn't I?'

'And I didn't intend to forgive you so easily, Miss Sue, but we've the rest of the day to spend together and I'm not much good at sign language.'

The touch of humour from him broke the tension and made her laugh shakily. 'Well, you usually give as good as is sent,' she couldn't resist retorting. 'All those doubtful "Miss Frazers" have the intended effect, which you know very well.'

What he might have replied was lost as they swung to an abrupt halt inside what looked to Sue like a ring of boulders, a natural car-park carved from the rock. 'Oh, lord,' she exclaimed, her eyes round, 'what a place!'

'It's the end of the track, where we leave all vehicles,' he explained. He looked down into her eyes for a second, searching them for panic. Finding only a lively interest, he nodded approvingly. 'From now on we use our legs, and the going is tough.'

The going *was* tough, although Sue would have died rather than complained. Besides, she found she was enjoying herself. Meric walked slightly in front, the rucksack containing their lunch slung on his back, and every now and again he paused to let her catch up. The morning mist still clung to the hillsides, but the mist didn't deter him, he knew the path well. The view as they climbed higher was beautiful – mountains, rocks, green valleys and sparkling burns. Sue, following closely, could hear the sound of running water, like music on the air. Presently the mist began to evaporate. A breeze sprang up, blowing the melting shreds of it away, and the hills stood out in bold ridges and jagged crests against the sharp blue sky.

An hour's solid climbing brought them out of the heather on to the bare hillside. It was hot and shadeless, so Sue was glad when they turned the shoulder of the hill and she felt the wind on her face. She felt inordinately grateful when Meric paused long enough to let her get a quick drink from one of the burns. The water tasted cool and fresh and very, very clean.

'Thirsty?' He gazed at her consideringly, noting the dark smudge across her wide brow where she had brushed back a tendril of hair with fingers soiled by contact with the rocks. His eyebrow quirked as he put out his own hand to flick off a fragment of sandy soil. 'At this rate,' he grinned, 'you'll need a wash as well as a drink!'

'I don't mind.' Refreshed, she looked back at him, returning his smile, her former antagonism forgotten in the exhilaration of the climb. Completely alive, her mind and body possessed by a mood of complete enthrallment with the wild country, she felt happier than she had done for some time. 'The air is marvellous. I could climb for hours without getting tired,' she said.

'Good.' Sardonically his eyes still lingered on her animated face as if held there by her lively expression. 'But we have yet some way to go. You aren't really big or tough enough for this sort of thing. You may be congratulating yourself too soon.'

Trust him to put a damper on things! 'So you require an

Amazon?' Her eyes sparked, the antagonism creeping back even while she strove to remain objective. It was probably women en masse he referred to, not just one inexperienced female like herself. A man like Meric Findlay would enjoy lumping everyone together. It was up to her to prove him wrong. 'An Amazon,' she repeated impatiently, moving beneath his fixed gaze as she waited his reply.

'I certainly don't require one, personally. It's the terrain I'm talking about, not me.' Tongue in cheek he grinned derisively as he turned away.

Exasperated, she picked up her anorak and followed. How did he always manage to have the last word!

They worked their way across the shoulder of the hill, climbing amongst rocks and scrambling down screes. The wind, which had been blowing on their faces, now swirled behind them, whistling through the narrow clefts with a strange moaning sound.

Sue shuddered, speaking to Meric's broad back. 'It's a bit eerie.'

He glanced around at her, nodding soberly. 'This is a grim sort of place. But, as you said before, the air is marvellous.' His dark eyes flicked across the stony ridges, the black boulders, the dark, bare clefts which sunlight never reached, gently mocking her delicate aversion.

'Where is the forest – the deer forest, I mean?' Unable to see even a single tree around or above them, Sue couldn't resist asking, even if it gave him another opportunity to tease.

Meric laughed as he eased his rifle on his shoulder. 'Didn't anyone tell you, Sue, there are no trees in a deer forest?'

Sue bit her lip as she walked on. It seemed she couldn't win. Up here, she felt and was totally ignorant. Small wonder he laughed at her!

'Never mind.' His glance took in her crestfallen face as his hand gently gripped her elbow. 'A lot of people make the same mistake. And don't ask me why it's called a forest. Very few of them ever have many trees.'

Feeling strangely grateful for his few kind words, Sue scrambled on. The track was very steep and stony, but presently it went around an outcrop of rock where it was blocked by a huge fall of stone. Meric had stopped and when she caught him up she saw that he had taken out his binoculars and was scanning the hills.

'Look, Sue,' he murmured, putting an arm out to draw her up close, 'there's a stag over there. Look over to Ben Cruan – he's at the entrance to the corrie. If we're lucky we'll get nearer, but first take these and see for yourself.'

Sue, too aware of his steadying arm, took the binoculars from him with hands which trembled slightly, focusing the instrument as he instructed on the wilderness in front of her. For a moment she could see nothing but bare hillside, but presently she caught sight of something brown that moved.

'Is it a stag?' she asked eagerly, straining to get a clearer view.

'Yes.' His arm tightened unconsciously, the line of his jaw taut as his eyes narrowed into the distance. 'It's a big one. We're too far off to see his points, but he's a big beast.'

'Can't we get nearer?' Impatiently she lowered the glasses, her gaze following his, but unable to see the stag without them.

'It's difficult.' Meric pointed out the steep decline covered with boulders and loose stones, the boggy patch in the bottom which lay between them and their quarry. 'The wind's in our favour,' he added in a low voice. 'This way it's blowing in our faces again so the stag can't get our scent. Deer, if you didn't know, have such a keen sense of smell they can scent a man from an incredibly long distance. But we're certainly going to try.'

With a quick, concentrating smile he put her from him, just as the warmth from his body was beginning to spread.

With a pang Sue realized that his gesture had been purely impersonal. So intent was he on the deer, he had scarcely realized she was there. Hastily she suppressed a sudden longing to stay within the circle of his arm as she dropped carefully behind him down the slope of the hill. As he had said, it was a difficult approach. If they were to dislodge a stone it could start a small avalanche which would warn the stag of their presence, but Sue found it difficult to move soundlessly over the uneven surface.

To her secret delight she did manage remarkably well, her quick, light movements matching Meric's experience, something which she sensed pleased him although he made no comment. His approval lay only in his brief smile as he turned his head to see how she was progressing. Soon they were down the slope, over the swampy patch at the bottom and climbing up the mountainside.

For a while they lost sight of the stag, but Meric told her he had marked the spot where he grazed. It was very still. In their present position they were sheltered, and nothing moved, not even a blade of grass. Sue, used as she was to city streets, had never known such silence. Then they were creeping slowly, mostly on their hands and knees, until eventually they were on a rocky ridge looking down into a narrow valley. A small burn ran down the middle of the valley, twisting amongst the stones, but there was no sign of the stag.

'He's moved to the upper part of the valley,' Meric whispered in her ear. 'Of that I'm certain. I know the corrie well and the grass at the top is sweet. He'll be feeding.'

'Are you sure?' Sue crawled up level with him, glancing anxiously sideways into his face. Unlike her own, his looked cool. Obviously he was hard, and in tip-top physical condition, as after the hard climb his breathing had scarcely altered. Feeling the hot perspiration on her brow, Sue glanced at him again, her eyes tinged with envy.

He was gazing straight across the incline and nodded his

head to her question. 'Yes. There's a passage between the burn and the mountainside, before the valley widens. Once past the burn the path is blocked by fallen rock, but we can climb on to a ridge and view him from above. Not a good angle to shoot him from, but then I'm not shooting today.'

They climbed down to the burn. It took several minutes, and as they drew nearer, Sue could see the passage between the burn and the cliff. She held her breath with excitement. Never before could she remember feeling like this, keyed up and brimming over with expectancy. And not a little, she acknowledged, had these feelings to do with the man beside her.

'Now we go up the cliff,' Meric said softly, beckoning to Sue to follow closely.

The rock was warm with the sun and the crevices were filled with grass and little pools of water. On some parts it was slippery and she didn't reject Meric's helping hand, but clung to it tightly, pulling herself up. Hot from exertion and quite without breath, she was thankful when they reached the top. Her hair tumbled in disorder about her face, and looking back she could see the woolly hat she had been wearing hooked on the branch of a stunted tree. She would collect it on the way down.

Meric drew her nearer, making way for her in a niche beside him. From their perch half-way up the mountain they could now see the top of the valley. It was small, filled with boulders, which Sue supposed had fallen from the higher crags. Between the boulders the grass looked fresh and green, surprising for the time of year. But it wasn't the grass which caught and held Sue's attention. It was the animal which grazed there completely unaware of the two watching strangers. It was a beautiful, brown-coloured, antlered stag.

CHAPTER EIGHT

IN her excitement Sue clutched Meric's arm, only just remembering to keep her voice down. 'What a beautiful beast!' she gasped, her eyes widening with admiration and something like awe. It was the first time in her life she had ever seen a stag apart from films and photographs, and she watched spellbound from her high perch on the rock. The animal was about a hundred yards away, grazing towards them head on, and even from that distance, she thought she could count ten points to his antlers.

She was right – as Meric confirmed. 'It's not a Royal stag. A Royal has twelve points to its antlers. But this one is very nice, about nine years old, I should think. You won't see anything much better.'

To let her have a better view he spread out his legs and settled his rifle against a piece of old turf. Sue lay down beside him, her eyes fixed on the corrie. The stag went on grazing. It was so still and sheltered in the corrie that she could hear the noise of the creature's hoof against the stones. He was coming nearer very slowly, seeking out the tender young grass between the boulders, still unaware of their presence.

'There may be more,' Meric whispered, easing himself more comfortably in the confined space. He was so near that glancing at him Sue saw herself reflected momentarily in the dark depth of his eyes. For a minute she was afraid to move or speak, to do anything to disturb her feelings of unreality. The length of his strongly muscled leg was pressed against her own, and when he spoke his breath came warm on her cheek. She stirred as a flicker of fire shot through her, distracting her attention from the animal in front of them.

Taking a deep breath, she said quickly, 'I suppose the

stags look more or less alike? Like sheep.'

He smiled at that. 'Don't make a remark like that near the shepherd – or our head keeper! He knows most of the stags by sight. We try to collect their horns and mark their development. They cast their horns every year, you see, and grow new ones. Once Donald and I had a set of horns from the same beast three years running. It was about eight years old. The horns showed a distinct improvement, although the number of points remained the same.'

Somehow it warmed Sue's heart to know that Meric wasn't just interested in the shooting, yet she couldn't stop herself asking, a hint of censoriousness in her voice, 'How do you choose which stags to kill?'

He grinned again, without rancour. 'Usually those with deformed horns, bad points. These are usually shot as they're not good to breed from. People sometimes refer to them as switches. Then there's another which we call a hummel – a beast without horns at all. Just hard, bony knobs where the horns should be, but he's usually big and heavy. All the same, we don't like the look of him.'

'I thought it was always a Royal stag that people went after?'

'Not always,' Meric shook his head. 'We don't shoot very many of those, but a chap the other day got one, a perfect twelve-pointer, well worth mounting. It's gone to the taxidermist in Dundee. But there again, the guests from the hotel don't always want to shoot. Like you, many of them just want to look and learn.'

Sue's eyes wavered and returned to the stag in the corrie. 'It wasn't until we came out,' she said, 'that I knew I was to be given the opportunity, Mr. Findlay.'

'Well, it's all part of the service,' he mocked smoothly.

The tone of his voice aroused resentment, and she turned sharply, not thinking, and dislodged a small stone. The sound of it falling was barely audible to the human ear, yet the stag below them stopped suddenly and raised its head, listening. His shining brown body turned sideways as he sniffed the air. Then before they could move he gave one bound towards the burn, springing across it with one incredible leap to disappear in seconds around the bottom of the valley. The swiftness of his leaving was almost unbelievable, and left Sue gasping.

Nothing else stirred in the silence. Meric stood up with abrupt grace, his kilt swinging. 'Now you can understand,' he teased, 'why a lot of people never get near them.'

Scrambling to her feet, Sue nodded, speechlessly. 'I suppose I've been lucky,' she agreed soberly.

'You could say that,' he conceded. 'You could also be grateful you were with such a good stalker.'

She looked back at him mischievously from beneath her lashes. 'I didn't think you were over-fond of gratitude, Mr. Findlay?'

She held his glittery, dark look. 'If you call me Mr. Findlay again, you'll never know what hit you, girl!'

Her mouth quirked in a careless smile which disregarded the menace in his face. 'You're full of dark threats today, aren't you? Most probably empty ones, but I don't scare easily.'

His light teasing provoked, but she doubted whether his mind was really on what he was saying, or her light responses. He was a busy man and quite likely regarded her as a bit of a nuisance, someone he could treat casually while he concentrated subconsciously on his current problems. Someone like a younger sister. Her own mind rebelled unexplainably at her inability to make any indelible impression. Illogical though it seemed, Sue decided, with feminine perversity, that she didn't like being ignored. It might not be wise, in fact it could be quite insane, but the desire was there in spite of his threats to provoke him a little in return!

He hadn't replied to her last remark, as with an indifferent shrug he turned and made his way back down into the valley, leaving her to follow as best she could. With one last wistful look towards the place where the stag had disappeared Sue scrambled after him, sliding down the cliff face to land in an undignified heap at his feet.

'Well, that's one way of doing it!' His eyebrows shot up and his voice drawled sardonically, and he made no attempt to help her to her feet.

She gazed at him scornfully as she picked herself up. Her hands were scratched where she had tried unsuccessfully to retain a grip on the rock, and one leg hurt slightly, but that would be nothing to him! A few well chosen words beat in her brain and it took a great effort to hold them in check. They would only bounce off his hard arrogance, she was sure of that. Even now, as she dusted herself down, he was picking up his coat and looking at his watch.

'We'll have something to eat,' he said, 'then it will be time to get back. It's almost two o'clock and we've some way to go.' With long strides he set off along the stony path. 'There's a good spot up here,' he told her over his shoulder. 'I've used it before. It's more comfortable than perching on a rock.'

Secretly intrigued, Sue trailed behind him up the burn, her movements freer now that the need for complete silence was past. As they went deeper into the small valley she found the isolation exciting. It might have been a private Shangri-la. They might have been explorers in some far off corner of the universe, trekking untrodden ground; the mountains of Tibet; the Great Wall of China. Vividly she allowed her imagination to run riot, through all the places she longed to see and probably never would. This place, she felt, was very old, sculptured in dramatic patterns by the elements, cut into jagged peaks and precipices by the sun and the rain and wind. A long, cold shiver ran down her spine as the thick isolation caught and held her, like a demon lover refusing to let go. Here a person could be lost for years before anyone might pass by. There must surely be ground here where no human foot had ever trod?

135

All too soon they came to the spot Meric had mentioned, a sheltered ring of boulders within the backdrop of mountains, and within the boulders, flat rock covered with grass. Grass, burnt and dried at this time of the year, but thick enough to provide some comfort in an otherwise barren landscape.

Meric turned. 'Will this do?' he asked, a slight smile at the corner of his mouth as he handed her the rucksack with the food.

Without waiting for her assent he placed his rifle against the cliff. She noticed how he always took the greatest care of it. Next he took off his waterproof jacket, spreading it for a pillow before he lay down. 'Now serve the food, woman,' he grunted as he stretched out his legs.

For a moment Sue's eyes dwelt indignantly on the whole long length of him, then, strangely submissive, she did as she was told. She tried to convince herself it was because he deserved it, not because he was so arrogant and good-looking that her heart could no longer resist him. It seemed the most natural thing in the world to work while he rested, to lay out the lunch Mrs. Lennox had provided. On a flat piece of exposed rock she put the ham sandwiches, the green apples, the thick wedges of home-made fruit cake and cheese. The flasks of coffee she put aside until the end of the meal, but removing the screw tops she went to the stream and scooped out two cups of the clear, sparkling water. If they were having ambrosia, food of the gods, then this surely would be nectar to go with it. Feeling enormously pleased with herself, she carried it back to their rocky table.

Meric opened his eyes as she sat down beside him, propping himself up on one elbow as she passed him a sandwich, noting her still damp cheeks which she had rinsed before returning from the burn. His gaze lingered appreciatively on the matt bloom on her skin before dropping slowly to the feast she had spread out. 'You'd make quite a good handmaiden,' he said amiably. 'In another age I might have purchased you.'

'I suppose,' Sue rejoined primly, 'I should feel flattered. You would have haggled over me in a market place?'

'I might have been tempted.'

'Provided the price wasn't too high?'

His eyes swept over her lazily, and her cheeks flushed at what she thought she read in his glance, something which smouldered there, causing a pulse to jerk in her throat. He laughed softly beneath his breath. 'You said that, not I, sweet Sue. In a moment of weakness you might tempt a man not to consider the cost.'

'But you would regret it later!' What foolishness made her persist with this inane conversation? It was like sliding down a precipice, once started one seemed unable to stop.

He continued to look at her, his expression sardonic. 'That would depend on several things, wouldn't it? The price of some things, Sue, is far beyond their true value.'

Quickly, to still a flicker of anger, she bit sharply into a green apple, crunching the white flesh with even white teeth. 'You don't like women much, do you, Meric?'

His eyes glinted, mocking her patent innocence. 'Of course I like women. You have a genius, Sue, for asking silly questions. Now, my opinion of them ...? Well, that's another matter altogether. I suppose you refer to women in general?'

What did he mean? With an almost physical effort she drew her eyes away from his enigmatical face. She wasn't going to ask him to elaborate. It would be wiser, she knew it instinctively, to change the subject. She shrugged her slim shoulders, suppressing a small yawn, deliberately giving the impression of boredom as her hand went out to a flask to pour coffee. Her appetite had suddenly gone, she wasn't even thirsty any more, but it was something to do and might distract his attention from her hot cheeks.

'I have enjoyed myself today,' she assured him, studiously polite as she measured brown sugar into his cup. She knew from experience that he took two spoonfuls. 'The stag was wonderful ... So is this place,' she tacked on haphazardly, staring around her.

He raised his eyebrows at her delicately tinted face, making it understood he was aware that she had ignored his last question. 'So much enthusiasm,' he murmured indifferently. 'I seem to have heard it all before.'

Of course he had! Crossly Sue flung herself on her back on the hot grass some feet away from him, preferring not to look at him. Guests from the hotel – women like herself from the cities. Their exaggerated expressions of delight would waft unheard about his cynical ears. 'It's known to be possible,' she retorted stubbornly, 'to fall in love with a place after only a short time.'

Lazily he put down his cup which he emptied in one long draught. His voice was soft but ironic. 'You're not cut out for places like this, Sue. You're sweet, and rather lovely, but don't try to fool yourself otherwise. Hothouse plants should stay in their proper environment, not seek to flourish where only the hardiest can survive.'

'I came with you here today! I kept up over all that rough ground, and you dare say that!'

Taking no notice of her indignant gasp, Meric rose to his feet, carried both their cups to the burn and rinsed them out. 'It's more like July than October,' he remarked quite casually. 'I've rarely known it so hot.'

Watching him from beneath her thick lashes as she lay on her back, Sue curved a hand compulsively around a hard piece of rock. Why did he enjoy raising a fine anger within her, such a turmoil of emotions she could never hope to sort out? 'You don't like me, do you?' she accused sharply. No sooner were the words out than she felt she had uttered them to him before.

'I don't think I do.' Noiselessly he turned to drop down lightly on the ground beside her. 'But liking needn't always enter into the relationship between a man and a woman, or don't you agree?' His eyes, clearly indicating his meaning, roved slowly over the curved outline of her young body. With an easy strength and without hurry, he pulled her into his arms, lying with her on the softly sensuous turf, one arm curved around her waist, the other beneath her head, his hand holding the fine bone of her shoulder.

A long time afterwards Sue wondered why she hadn't attempted to escape. Afterwards she blamed the heat which partly drugged her senses, and the atmosphere with its almost hypnotical silence. The feeling that Meric Findlay and she were quite alone in the world, and what was happening was a natural continuation of the pleasure she had experienced in the morning.

She did stir, not wanting to after a long moment, yet subtly aware of the danger of staying where she was. But with easy strength he controlled her first tentative movement, his hand tightening slightly on her shoulder, his chin pressing just a little more firmly on the top of her head.

'Be still,' he ordered, his voice low, lazily indifferent, as he stretched his long legs out against her. 'You told me before you were grateful!'

But that didn't mean ...? Somehow, when she tried to speak, the words stuck in her throat. A curious inertia which she had felt before in his arms seemed to be taking over, rejecting any desire to protest. He was holding her gently, as if seeking to reassure her, almost as if she were one of the small animals of the forest which he held captive in his embrace. She said, because she felt she must, 'Do you always exact payment in this fashion?'

He laughed deep in his throat. 'I can't think of anything more gratifying.'

She was silent, turning the word over in her mind, not liking the sound of it. She was aware that he could, if he wished, be utterly ruthless, that he was too dangerous to play with, and yet she didn't care. It could be an opinion that by appearing totally acquiescent she was inviting trouble, but the experimental rapport of just lying in Meric's arms seemed curiously irresistible. After all, it was just for a few minutes, it wasn't necessary to go any further. At twenty-one it was perhaps time she began to live a little more dangerously, to lose a little of her former inhibition. No man would want an inexperienced schoolgirl. If only, she thought, with a small despairing sigh, she had a few guidelines to go by!

Unexpectedly he raised himself on one elbow, traces of a question on his dark face as he looked down at her. 'Why the sigh, sweet Sue? Are you wondering how you're going to cope?' The timbre of his voice was amused and sardonic, stiffening her diminishing resistance.

'I'm not wondering anything of the sort,' she lied lightly. Attempting to substantiate her statement, she glanced directly into his eyes, a warm wave of air dancing between them, but her faint little smile never quite made it. Something in his expression made her tilt her face defiantly, and her smile faded as a dark wave of apprehension washed over her, as softly and very gently he lowered his lips to hers.

The touch of his lips was like fire going through her, but before she could free herself his hand slid under her hair and pinned the nape of her neck. Carefully the pressure of his mouth increased as his fingers moved back to her hair, raking through it slowly, gently smoothing the heavy silkiness of it from her forehead and ear. Her head seemed to swim at the warm crush of his mocking mouth on hers. As he drew her sensuously closer, his heavy body held hers to the heady scent of the crushed grass. Flushed and tormented, her fair head thrown back, she returned his exploring kisses with a kind of helpless hunger.

Something within her leapt crazily, jerking through her being, a whirlpool of emotion, striving for expression. Involuntarily her arms went up around his neck, her fingers threading through the dark thickness of his hair, as his own hands went down to linger hard on her waist before going up under her blouse to rest, his fingers wide-spread over the soft skin on her back.

Then suddenly his mouth eased slowly from her own, just enough to allow her to draw one deep shuddering breath.

'Poor Sue,' he murmured, his mouth trailing fire across her face, holding her to him as she tried to draw back, his lips dropping to the soft hollow in her throat. 'And you thought you could cope!'

His words stung through the flame which threatened to consume her. His voice was low but as sardonic as before, as he mocked her inability to fight the wilfulness of her devastated emotions.

'I might, if you let me go,' she gasped unsteadily. 'If it wasn't for your brute strength . . .'

His eyes glittered as he dropped another brief kiss on her lips. 'Must you always seek excuses, Sue? You'll be telling me next you have a built-in aversion to this sort of thing.'

'Not exactly.' Through a haziness of mind Sue thought it better to stick to half-truths. 'It rather depends who I'm with.'

'Tim Mason, for instance?' One of his hands left the warm flesh of her back and returned to her throat, encircling it forcibly. 'I wonder – are you usually such a liar?'

'You don't believe me, then?' she asked, helpless under his infinitely exciting touch.

'The devil I do!' he muttered thickly, and drew her savagely to him again, this time parting her lips with the force of his own.

Regardless now of what he thought, Sue returned his kisses eagerly, frightened yet revelling in the tide of feeling which was rising between them. Her body went soft and curiously boneless against his, and his hand moved across her back, gripping the bare skin, inflicting a fine pain which shot through to her breast, moving her lips in a wide little gasp under his own. Crushed against him, she clung to him feverishly, losing all awareness of everything but the needs of her pulsing, hungry body.

He could feel her trembling, and lifted his dark head fractionally, muttering against her lips, 'Just how permissive were you in that college of yours, dear Sue?'

'It doesn't matter . . .' Through the thick drumming of her heart Sue heard herself answer, again diverting from the truth, filled with a crazy desire to stay in his arms. If she confessed her innocence, he wouldn't want her, and, in a moment of insanity she knew she wanted him, as she'd never wished for anything in her life before!

'Sue!' For a long moment she imagined she was to get what she desired. As the closeness of their bodies became charged with tension, she tried to hide the torment in her eyes. All her life she had waited for this, a moment when she might let her mind sink beneath mounting sensation. And, as he roughly spoke her name and his mouth hardened on hers again, her doubts faded against a wave of feeling so intense that she had no wish to fight it.

'Darling,' she whispered, beneath her breath, but the soft sound she made must have reached him. In an instant he lifted his head, seeming to retreat from her as with one fluid movement he rose to his feet.

Quickly he pulled her up with him, still holding her, but lightly, waiting until she recovered some form of balance. His voice came, faintly indulgent if very dry. 'What did you expect this time, sweet Sue?'

Transfixed and blazing blue, her eyes fastened on him, all the turmoil inside her reflected in the colour which flared across her white face. 'I hate you!' she cried, attempting furiously to defy him, truly hating his male arrogance, even while she longed to be back in his arms.

'No, you don't.' Remorselessly his fingers bit into her arm, keeping her still. 'But you might do if we stayed here longer. Grow up a little, for God's sake, Sue!'

Her slight figure seemed to droop on his arm. 'I don't think this conversation is doing either of us any good.' Her

142

voice came low, tinged with strain and a gathering bewilderment.

Meric's mouth quirked, but his smile held no mirth. 'You would never have forgiven me, Sue. You might even have said that I deliberately tried to compromise you in order to get the estate, that I was trying to keep the heiress chained to my side.'

His lips, which had been so gently persuasive just a few minutes ago, tightened as she stared at him, and he felt her body stiffen. 'You can't be serious?' she choked.

For a brief space of time something in her face seemed to hold him oddly, then with a grin he said suavely, shattering still further all her preconceived little notions, 'I suppose we're really a couple of fools, Sue, and neither of us too pleased with the other. I certainly didn't mean to hurt you intentionally – but let it pass. Nothing will have changed came the morning. In any case, we must get going if we hope to make Glenroden before dark. I don't think you'd really enjoy spending the night with me out here!'

Feeling distinctly chilled, she followed him along the burn, on to the rough downhill track where she had almost to run to keep up with his loose-limbed stride. Unhappily she stared at his broad back, scarcely aware of where she was walking. Never could she remember feeling so deflated. On the mountain, protected in Meric's arms against the elements, she hadn't cared at all about getting back to Glenroden, but now all she felt she wanted was somewhere to hide her head. She could only feel grateful that at least he didn't know how much his rejection hurt.

The Range-Rover was waiting for them as they reached the lower ground again. To her surprise, after putting their gear in the back, Meric actually came around and opened the door for her to help her in. With one foot on the step she turned swiftly to look at him. Tall and rugged as the country around them, he was handsome in a compelling sort of way –

his quick observant eyes, his firm mouth and determined-looking jaw, his hair, thick and vital and very dark. She knew in that instant that she loved him and quickly she lowered her heavy lashes, that he shouldn't, with his keen perception, read what must surely lie behind them. If nothing else it brought a grain of comfort that her behaviour in the corrie hadn't been completely wanton. That it had been evoked by an emotion as old as Eve, stronger than one inexperienced girl. But momentarily stunned by the knowledge of her own involvement, she remained quite still. There was no way in which she could possibly tell him, so she must be prepared that he should think the worst. Maybe better this than he should know the truth, and be amused by it?

'A penny for them, Sue?' He was waiting to close the door, his brows raised sardonically but his eyes curious.

'Not for sale,' she managed to reply briefly, a faint smile touching her curved lips which still felt bruised from the pressure of his.

'From the expression on your face,' he said, 'I thought they might be interesting.'

'I suppose I was day-dreaming,' she admitted. 'Anyway, it wasn't important.'

To her surprise he suddenly grinned, his eyes alight with laughter, but for once his laughter sounded kind.

'Maybe tomorrow I'll ask you to be more explicit, Sue. But right now we must get a move on, or John will be worrying. And he did trust me to look after you safely,' he pointed out amiably.

So amiably that Sue's heart gave a small lurch in her breast. He was in good spirits over something and not troubling to hide it. Maybe – the thought was fleeting, but it brought her gaze back to his face – maybe after all he did like her a little? There seemed to be a promise in his laughter about which she dared not begin to think. Instead she nodded cautiously, but made no comment as he gently closed the door and climbed in beside her.

It was getting dark as they reached home, the colour fading from the west, but as they passed the loch there was still a flare of red across the water against the darkening sky. There seemed a strange savagery about the land bathed in this half-light which made Sue shudder in spite of the warmth of her thoughts. Autumn was a nostalgic time of year in the country, when the heather was fading and the leaves turning colour. In the whispering morning mists and the shadowed clouds across the hills there was sadness, a brooding, a feeling of finality as the seasons drew to a close. Unpredictably she felt hot tears stinging the back of her eyelids, tensing her throat, until it was almost with a cry of relief that she saw they were back at Glenroden.

'I'll go straight in and see Father,' she said quickly as they left the Range-Rover. 'He's probably been lonely without us.'

But in thinking this she was wrong, and afterwards she wished fervently that their homecoming could have been different.

Mrs. Lennox met them at the door, or near it, as she was just coming down the great oak staircase. 'Oh, it's glad I am to see you back,' she cried rather nervously. 'You have a visitor, Susan, a Mr. Mason, and I wasn't quite sure what to do with him.'

Behind her Sue felt the rigidness of Meric's hand which had been resting lightly on her waist as he walked with her to the house. It had been nothing, she assured herself, but a friendly gesture, but from it she had derived great comfort, an indefinable sense of happiness. Now, for a split second, as his fingers bit into the curve of her hip, she sensed his anger and restraint.

His hand dropped sharply and she felt bereft. Tim couldn't surely be here? And yet he must be, as Mrs. Lennox was adding quickly, 'He came early after lunch and seemed quite put out that you weren't here, Susan. However, your

145

father and he have been getting on like a house on fire, talking their heads off all afternoon. I've prepared a room. I've just shown Mr. Mason up, as a matter of fact. He'll be staying, of course. At least Mr. Frazer said he thought so.'

'Of course,' Meric was nodding smoothly by her side. 'Susan's boy-friend is very welcome. I hope you made that clear, Mrs. Lennox?'

As he spoke dismay flooded through Sue, tightening the nerves of her stomach, fading the pink glow of her cheeks. It was no use suggesting there had been a mistake, that it might not be Tim, when instinctively she knew it could be no one else. But why, why had he come all the way to Glenroden? At this moment he was the last person on earth she wanted to see. Carefully, aware of the pregnant silence, she moistened dry lips before asking Mrs. Lennox, 'Did he say why he's here? What he wanted?' which sounded ungracious and slightly stupid, and which would have been better left unsaid. Only something in Meric's face as he stood regarding her grimly prompted her to indiscretion.

Before Mrs. Lennox could reply he murmured ironically, 'You shouldn't ask foolish questions, Sue. Obviously the fellow couldn't wait, and I repeat, he's welcome to stay a few days if he feels like it. In fact,' his eyes narrowed consideringly, 'it might not be such a bad idea, providing he behaves himself.'

The arrogance in his tone stung Sue as she gazed up at him. He was like a stranger, not the man who had held her in his arms on the wild mountainside, who had given the impression on the way home that their relationship had moved subtly to a different level. Now she could only stare at him with a leaden heart as involuntarily she tried to excuse Tim's behaviour. 'Tim probably had a spell of leave due and thought he'd surprise me. He wouldn't realize that it mightn't be convenient.'

Mrs. Lennox interrupted, glancing quickly from one to the other. 'It's no inconvenience, Susan, so don't let that worry you. If Mr. Findlay doesn't mind, I'm sure we'll never notice the extra work.'

'It need not concern Mr. Findlay!' Again words tripped indiscreetly off Sue's tongue. It wasn't what she'd meant to say at all.

'Sue!' Meric's brief exclamation hit her sharply as, confused, she turned to go. Startled, she looked back at his face, noting that he seemed to go white beneath his tan. She was also aware that but for Mrs. Lennox's presence he might have lost his temper. Instead he pushed derisively past her, striding to the far side of the hall. Over his shoulder he said tautly, 'Another time you feel like entertaining, please let us know beforehand. If only for your father's sake,' he added, as if under compulsion.

But it seemed that Tim's visit to Glenroden didn't have an adverse effect. At least, not on John Frazer. John, in fact, seemed to enjoy his company, and the two men often talked or just sat together for long periods. Sue realized with a pang that their friendship, though in some ways surprising, had developed easily. There were none of the somewhat forced attempts to find something more permanent than a friendly camaraderie, none of the sometimes uncomfortable straining after a deeper, more lasting relationship which plagued Sue's own daily contact with her father. As Meric had pointed out, it was maybe because they were both too impatient, but, apart from their shared pleasure over John's book, nothing seemed to be changing very rapidly. Hearing John talking and laughing so easily with Tim seemed to emphasize her unspoken doubts – that the gap caused by the missing years was too wide ever to properly bridge. And unless something changed she could never feel a genuine daughter of the household, or be willing to accept any part of Glenroden should anything happen to John.

Tim, however, was plagued by no such doubts. Like her father he seemed continually amazed by her likeness to the Frazers, and never missed an opportunity of noting this aloud. Like her father, when she had first come, he never seemed to tire of arranging her in front of one of the many family paintings, or of contriving to go with her through the heavy family albums of Frazer photographs, pointing out how in both figure and face she resembled them closely.

'There's no doubt about it, Susan,' he exclaimed, on his third morning at Glenroden, as they stood together in the drawing room, held there, unwilling prisoners by the wind and rain outside. 'It's quite clear to see that you're a Frazer all right! It was a good move when I allowed you to come here. Anyway, John has been telling me his solicitor has verified it through and through, so there can be no mistake. Just look at your grandmother's picture. There's no question about it at all!'

Rather blindly Sue stared up into her grandmother's face, wondering if she imagined a slightly enigmatic smile. Tim did go on so! Half-heartedly she nodded and shrugged. Why should she feel a twinge of resentment that Tim should call her father by his first name so easily? Her father preferred it, she knew, but Tim might have desisted for a little while. She also knew a twinge of resentment that he should have so easily gained John's confidence. Already, after only two days, Tim seemed in possession of more facts concerning Glenroden than she herself was after all this time? Already, too, John seemed to have the impression that she and Tim were to be married, and try as she might he appeared to think that her protests just amounted to a schoolgirlish embarrassment.

'I know you're right, Tim,' she answered, a trifle impatiently, 'but please don't go on about it! You never let us forget for a minute, and it gets a bit tiresome, don't you think? It's as if you're trying too hard to convince somebody.'

'That manager chap, for instance?' Tim's face grew sullenly-determined. 'I rather think I could put him in his place if I were here long enough.'

'But you've only two weeks ... At least, that is what you said?' Sue's brow creased anxiously. 'And I'm not really sure of Meric's position ...'

'Then it's time someone was!' Tim's voice held an oddly threatening note, and Sue's breath caught in her throat. Unaccountably she felt a little shiver of fear. The face Tim turned to her seemed stiff with determination.

'Please,' she whispered, staring at him as she tried to marshal her thoughts. His attitude filled her with a growing apprehension, making it impossible to deny that since he came she had been unable to relax. Again and again she found herself wishing he hadn't been here at all. This late holiday which he hadn't expected to collect owing to the pressure of work was, so far as she was concerned, turning out to be a fiasco. As she had guessed, he had intended surprising her by arriving unannounced, and had obviously not even noticed her lukewarm welcome. He had been much too busy making himself pleasant to John and Mrs. Lennox. Meric he treated coolly, with the offhand politeness of an important visitor towards a lower member of the staff, and at times Sue found herself cringing helplessly at the tone of voice he employed.

'Well – please what?' Tim prompted impatiently as she hesitated.

With a start she pulled herself together. 'What I meant to say, Tim, is that you mustn't start interfering. Meric Findlay, in many ways, is indispensable. You haven't had much time to realize this, but do try to remember in future. My father wouldn't be very pleased if you did anything to upset him.'

'So . . .' Tim's eyes narrowed suspiciously on her flushed face, and she noticed with confusion that he seemed relatively unimpressed. 'I'm beginning to wonder,' he went on shrewdly, 'who would be the most upset! But don't get all hot and bothered, Susan. I'm only trying to look after your interests.'

'I haven't,' she retorted, her chin tilting indignantly, 'any interests to look after, Tim. So please don't . . .'

'Don't what . . .?' he mimicked suavely. 'Don't upset the great Meric Findlay, you mean? Are you scared of him, Susan, or what? It seems to me,' his eyes gleamed suddenly beneath his sandy lashes, 'that you're almighty anxious to keep on the right side of him!'

'Just because we couldn't run Glenroden without him!' Sue insisted. 'Of course I'm not scared of him! You get such ridiculous ideas, Tim. I rarely see the man.' Which wasn't so far from the truth, she thought miserably. Meric had scarcely been near her, other than at mealtimes, at which he now chose to appear regularly. But for the most part he seemed to ignore her, apart from the barest of civilities – a state of affairs which might only have coincided with Tim's arrival, having more to do with the incident on the mountain. Anything Tim might say or do obviously couldn't make things worse as far as she was concerned, but for John's sake she must try to retain the modicum of politeness he still showed towards her.

Preoccupied, she watched Tim moving thoughtfully around the room, examining closely the fine paintings, the valuable objets d'art which filled the antique cabinets and decorated the mantelshelf of the beautiful Adam fireplace.

'There are other men,' he said sharply, 'who would be quite capable of running an estate like Glenroden. Once we're married, Susan, I shall probably see about getting someone more congenial.'

'I'm sure you would!' Furiously, her voice laced

with sudden sarcasm, Sue spun away from him, only to suppress a startled gasp as she heard a small noise in the doorway. Carlotte Craig was standing there gazing at them.

CHAPTER NINE

How long had Carlotte been standing there? Sue, the pink in her cheeks deepening to red, put a hasty hand to her face in a futile attempt to hide her embarrassment. Carlotte, however, was smiling quite gaily, and gave no indication that she had overheard anything, but with Carlotte one could never be quite sure. Sue could only hope fervently that she had only arrived in that second.

'Aren't you going to introduce me to your friend?' With raised brows, Carlotte obviously waited, her glance going past Sue to rest curiously on Tim's equally speculative face.

Somehow Sue managed to perform the small ceremony with dignity, but her mind was anything but cool as she watched Tim shake Carlotte's hand, his face full of expansive cordiality. Her thoughts flew angrily back to what he had been saying when Carlotte arrived. How dared he put her in such a spot, assuming so loudly that she was willing and eager to marry him? Why, oh, why hadn't she said definitely no in London, instead of not taking him seriously? The sooner she straightened things out the better, but it was scarcely possible to do so in front of another person.

Uneasily she realized Carlotte was probing blatantly, her brilliant smile covering a determination to discover Tim's exact status. 'You're Susan's boy-friend from London, I suppose? I didn't quite catch what she said.'

'Well, you could say that,' Tim answered, before Sue could speak. 'Actually I'm rather hoping to be something more, but there's nothing official at the moment, you understand?'

'Of course,' Carlotte agreed smoothly. Obviously, by the way her smile widened, the news suited her more than a little. 'I've just returned from London myself,' she confided with a charming grimace. 'I must confess to feeling rather flat, but this spot of romance has cheered me up considerably. Have you and Susan known each other long?'

'Oh, yes.' Tim was not reluctant. 'We've known each other a long time. I looked after Susan and her mother, you might say. We lived near each other, and her mother was always glad of my advice.'

When she gets Tim alone, Sue thought desperately, she'll be asking all sorts of questions. Yet how could she do anything to avert it when there wasn't really anything particular to hide? Tim's only fault was perhaps that he was too impulsive, that he had construed a situation incorrectly. It had nothing to do with his basically generous self. It was probably more her fault than his that he was here. She had been mistaken in thinking that once out of sight he would automatically forget her. And now that he was here how could she possibly ask him to go?

Confused, she brushed a strand of hair back from her hot brow. Carlotte was still smiling, apparently well pleased with herself. Instinctively, in spite of her friendly demeanour, Sue distrusted that smile, and her uneasiness increased as Carlotte suggested blandly:

'We must all get together one evening and go down to the hotel. Meric will know the best night to go. Perhaps we might have something official to celebrate by then. You never know!'

What did she mean? Sue blinked, her eyes wide and startled as dismay flooded her heart. Was she hinting, not perhaps at Tim, but at some relationship between Meric and herself? 'I'll keep it in mind,' she replied cautiously, trying to appear gracious. 'It will all depend how John is.'

'And that reminds me,' Carlotte nodded her head agreeably, 'it was John whom I really came to see. How is he?'

On safer ground, Sue found herself assuring her that her father was fairly well. 'He was talking to Meric a short while ago,' she said, not thinking.

'Oh, good!' Satisfied with the news, Carlotte turned to go, a smug smile on her dark red lips. 'I've arranged to go with Meric to Perth this morning,' she explained. 'He's going to a livestock sale. I'm returning with him this evening and staying to dinner, so I'll see you both then.'

With a light lift of one hand she was gone, leaving them both staring silently after her.

Tim was the first to find his tongue. 'At least she appears to be a girl with a head on her shoulders,' he spoke appreciatively as they heard her opening and closing John's door a little further along the hall. 'Certainly she seems to know what side her bread's buttered on – or is she just busy buttering it?' he joked rudely.

'Tim! I wish you wouldn't talk like that,' Sue pleaded stiffly, not knowing how much more of it she could stand. Her head ached. 'I'm sure Carlotte has no ulterior motives. She just pays friendly visits. Actually,' she added, 'she helps to run the caravan park in summer, so we see quite a bit of her.'

'Caravan park?' Tim's official ears pricked. 'Whose is the caravan park, might I ask?'

'Not if you use that tone of voice you may not,' Sue retorted coldly. 'It's on the estate, so I suppose it's ours, but it's all legal and above board, with a proper office and facilities and that sort of thing. So you needn't be suspicious!'

'Susan, do be quiet,' he interrupted sharply, looking slightly affronted. 'I wasn't even hinting at such a thing. I only intended pointing out that a caravan site can be a real asset as well as a lucrative means of profit if properly run, as you say this one is.'

Restively Sue glanced at him, a tiny frown between her winged brows, wondering, not for the first time, why she couldn't think faster. Tim saw things which never occurred to an ordinary individual. With him it was second nature, something which made him good at his job, and quick to

154

gain promotion. But to Sue, who usually accepted things on face value, it wasn't so easy to delve beneath the surface.

'On a place like this,' she said at last, 'one thing usually balances another. The caravan park and other enterprises, such as deer-stalking, must help subsidize the lack of profit from other parts of the land.'

'Deer-stalking, too?' Tim looked up quickly from his examination of a small Canton enamel dish. 'It seems to me, Susan, that you could be heir to quite a property, one way and another. Have you ever been right round the estate? Have you any idea what size it is?'

Mutely Sue shook her head, wishing distractedly she could find the courage to tell Tim to mind his own business. Yet it might be foolish to allow him to disturb her so deeply. But how to shut him up without being rude? Perhaps the wisest way to divert him would be to use a little diplomacy?

'I have been deer-stalking,' she said listlessly. 'Remember, I was out with Meric on the day you arrived.'

Tim leaned forward. 'Doesn't it seem strange that this was the first time you'd been out on the estate, in two months?'

'Not really.' Sue moved away from him, hoping he hadn't noticed the uncertainty in her eyes. Not easily could she confess to thinking the same thing herself. His questions echoed to closely her own doubts. Helplessly she tried to push them aside. 'You see, Tim, Father is far from well, and I don't want to do anything to upset him – or Meric Findlay.'

'Upset?' Out of sympathy, Tim stuttered crossly, 'I can understand about your father. Actually, I like him a lot, old girl. But, regarding Meric Findlay, it's up to you to assert yourself a little, or you'll be trodden into the dust!' Taking no notice of her small protesting gasp, he continued, 'Didn't your cousin Carlotte say that she and dear Findlay are off to Perth for the day? Well, while they're away, how about you and me having a look around? Just see if you can get hold of a map, John must have one somewhere, and I'll do the rest. It's amazing what can be ferreted out with the aid of a good map and a little ingenuity.'

'But, Tim . . .' Not liking his tone, Sue glanced back at him, startled. 'I shouldn't feel happy doing all this behind Father's back, so to speak.'

'But we're not doing any harm, and no one need know, if it will make you feel any better,' Tim argued. 'Besides, if the others are out enjoying themselves, why shouldn't you?'

Tim was goading her deliberately, Sue realized this. But when she reluctantly agreed to do as he suggested, it had nothing to do with the motive he had uppermost in mind. It was the thought of Meric and Carlotte spending the day together that prompted her to give her assent. She knew, in a moment of truth, that she couldn't bear to be here brooding about them until they returned. And, as Tim said, there could surely be no harm in exploring the estate. When one thought about it rationally, perhaps he was right. She should have been taken around sooner.

In the end, however, it wasn't altogether easy to approach her father, especially when she found it impossible to be completely frank. 'I would just like to show Tim the district,' she told him, when she went to his room. 'I was wondering if you had a map of the area. Perhaps one showing the boundaries of Glenroden, just so I can point them out?'

A curious expression flitted across John's tired face as he eased himself up in his bed. It wasn't one of his good days. Carlotte, he said, had wearied him with her chatter, and he didn't seem disposed to talk any more. Sensitive to his moods, Sue decided that if nothing else, it would be a good thing to take Tim away for a little while – while John rested. It was obvious, though, that he didn't seem very pleased by her request for a map, and she wondered if he would rather she stayed by his side. But he refuted the idea when she put her doubts into words, although he still didn't appear very happy about her previous suggestion.

'You'd have been better,' he said testily, 'to have gone with Carlotte to Perth. There would have been more of interest to you there. I think Meric has most of the maps in the office, but if you look in the top drawer of that cabinet over there you might find a small one.'

'I could always get one from the office, I suppose.' Sue looked at the map dubiously when she found it. It was faded and somewhat tattered, and she could see at a glance that it wouldn't be much help.

'No, don't do that!' Her father surprised her by speaking quite sharply. 'Don't ever go there, Susan, without asking Meric first. I mean,' he added, oddly hesitant, 'I wouldn't like you disturbing anything and perhaps giving him extra work.'

'No, of course not.' Sue, her eyes anxiously on his pale face, thought it better not to argue. 'I won't go near the office, but if you could just point out the boundaries on this, then we'll be off. The rain has stopped, I can see.'

John, however, had turned away from her on to his side as if he couldn't be bothered. 'Just go, Susan, please. There are plenty of places you can visit without getting lost. Meric took you up the mountain, but I wouldn't advise you going there today. If you were to get lost you'd soon find that Tim Mason is no Meric Findlay,' he finished enigmatically.

Feeling slightly hurt, Sue departed. Why was her father always so reluctant to explain anything about Glenroden? It wasn't as if she was ever very curious or probed, but if it was mortgaged up to the hilt, or something equally disastrous, he had only to tell her. Many estates went through bad times; it was nothing to be ashamed of. If it was something like this, at least it would squash her niggling suspicions that his secrecy had something to do with Meric. A transitory wave of self-pity smote her, as she went to collect her coat. Why couldn't John consider her position more? It wasn't easy when her heart refused to believe that Meric could do anything wrong, but her common sense told her otherwise.

'We'll take the Mini,' she told Tim. 'I still have it as one day I intend to get a job and will need it. The car, I mean,' she tacked on hastily. She didn't intend telling him that she needed a job rather desperately for some spare cash. He would only laugh.

Tim, fortunately, was too busy perusing the map to pay much attention to what she was saying. She doubted if he had even heard. To her surprise he was smiling in an altogether satisfied manner. Apparently, to him, the age and shabbiness of the map was no deterrent. 'You ought to be keeping your eye on this little lot,' he exclaimed, tapping the faded lines with one finger, 'and not worrying about a job! As far as I can see your father owns a huge stretch of territory. No wonder Mr. Findlay doesn't want you to know.'

'Tim, please!' In her agitation Sue changed gear too quickly on a corner, jerking them forward in their seats. 'I'm sorry,' she muttered through Tim's warning shout. 'But please don't agitate me any more. If you insist on going on about Meric, then I'm going home!'

'Okay, calm down.' Tim's eyebrows rose unrepentantly. 'You know your mother relied on me to look after your interests. I'm only trying to point out one or two things, as I did before. It isn't impossible, nor would it be the first time, that a man in your father's state of health has been taken advantage of.'

Sue remained mutinously silent. It was bad enough thinking things herself without having him put them into words. They were passing the river ford on their way to the loch, and Tim insisted on getting out at the caravan park.

'Just for a quick look,' he said, ignoring her glum face with a smooth smile. 'I might even come here on holiday myself.' He ran an expert eye across the near row of vans.

158

Wincing, Sue watched him wandering about, her gaze straying behind him to the loch where the light wind blew ripples across the deep water. Where larch and pine flanked the white-sanded shore and the sky hung cloudless above it. Now that the rain had gone, the clearing skies would bring frost, a first taste of winter, and Sue shivered. What was winter like in the Highlands? she wondered. In her mind's eye she saw the long, dark evenings, the cosy log fires, the isolation which must surely be part of winter in these parts. Her own position at Glenroden might be obscure, but such a picture more than made up for any feelings of insecurity. Winter here meant Meric and John, and Mrs. Lennox. She refused to think about Carlotte – and Tim would be gone.

When Tim returned from his tour of the caravans he seemed in excellent spirits and for the rest of the day remained in a good mood. Afterwards Sue was never quite sure how far they went. Tim, to her surprise, proved a first-class map reader, seemingly quite capable of guiding her through the wildest of places. If it hadn't been for the faint, unexplainable uneasiness at the back of her mind she might almost have enjoyed herself.

At one place the road, no more than a rough track, went up through a sort of rocky canyon, running close to the edge of a deep ravine where they seemed to cling precariously to the cliff wall, and as they looked back they could see nothing but the tops of firs and the gleam of bright water far below.

'You'd better keep your eyes on the road,' Tim remarked dryly, as Sue caught her breath. 'We should be nearly at the top, but I want to get there, not to the bottom again!'

On top the view proved well worth the perilous journey.

Beyond the loch, beyond the ridges, the background of mountains looked across at them, magnificent against the skyline. After careful consideration Sue decided she could see the mountain which she and Meric had climbed after the stag.

She told Tim about it. 'It really was a wonderful experience,' she said, and wondered why he gave her a funny look.

They walked back to the car which they'd left on the track. 'Just a little further on,' said Tim, putting a friendly arm about her shoulders, 'we dip back down to the main road, then back to Glenroden. Are you satisfied with your day today?'

'Umm.' Not paying much attention, Sue glanced at him uncertainly. It seemed rather an odd way of putting it, but she supposed she was. 'I've enjoyed the run around, if that's what you mean,' she found herself saying. 'And I should never have managed it myself.'

'This is what I've been trying to tell you,' he declared with emphasis. 'I know we don't see eye to eye about many things, but at least allow me to guide you in some. I don't want to see you hurt.'

She gazed back at him blankly. 'Hurt?' she repeated.

'Oh, never mind. It doesn't matter!' Appearing completely exasperated by her lack of co-operation, he slammed the car door. 'Sometimes I wonder, Susan, if you're being deliberately obtuse. It doesn't do to place too much trust in the wrong person.'

'Well, that's plain common sense, of course, and I've surely got enough of that?' Sue tried to keep the conversation in a lighter vein, but wasn't sure she had succeeded when he asked abruptly:

'Has John always been ill?'

Unprepared for his question, Sue replied with some confusion. 'Yes. At least I think so, for these last few years at any rate. That's what Doctor McRoberts told me. When I first arrived he'd hurt his ankle – Father, I mean, and that very same night he had a bad heart attack. He hasn't really properly recovered since. Doctor McRoberts did say that the ankle and my turning up unexpectedly might have been culminating factors.'

'This Doctor McRoberts doesn't beat about the bush.'

'I know, Tim, but I did ask him, and he gave me an honest answer. It wasn't any use avoiding the issue anyway. I knew it was partly my fault. This is why I mustn't be the cause of any further upset. It's important to me that Father doesn't suffer any more on my account.'

'Enough said . . .' Tim shrugged impatiently. 'You always did make a habit of blaming yourself for everything! I should have thought, regarding the circumstances, that you'd find it easier to settle down if you had everything cut and dried.'

'In what way?' Sue's own voice was ringed with impatience.

'Well, if I were you, I should make one definite attempt to regularize the situation without worrying John. There must be an agreement somewhere concerning Meric Findlay, possibly in the office, not even tucked out of sight. If you could find it, then you might know exactly how things stood. This estate is large, and I think with your father so ill you ought to feel some responsibility.'

Meric had rung while they were away. Mrs. Lennox had answered the telephone, and he had told her that Carlotte and he were staying in Perth to dine with friends. The same friends would run him home afterwards.

'It would save Miss Craig a journey,' Mrs. Lennox quoted. 'Fortunately,' she added, 'I hadn't started to prepare anything, but then Mr. Findlay is always very considerate.'

He isn't always, Sue muttered, half aloud, as she went upstairs to bed. After a light supper she had decided to have an early night, and had left Tim listening to the radio. There was no television at Glenroden. Meric made love to her, then scarcely spoke for days. He roused her feelings so that she couldn't rest, and expected her to continue as if nothing had happened. So far as he was concerned probably nothing had! Men! She shrugged, with the careless lift of her shoulders attempting to hide an aching heart. How foolish she had been to imagine she could spend the winter at Glenroden. She would never survive! She must remember to ask Carlotte if she had heard anything more about the teaching vacancy she had mentioned. It might be necessary to get away sooner than she had thought.

A few days later Meric surprised her by announcing at breakfast that he had booked a table for four, for the following evening. 'There's a hotel near Pitlochry,' he said, unsmilingly, 'which I think you might enjoy. Usually on a Saturday evening there's entertainment of a sort thrown in.'

Tim perked up immediately, almost prepared to be civil. 'It will make a change,' he agreed. 'Susan and I would like to go.'

Although Meric had addressed her, Tim obviously took it for granted that he was included in the invitation. In spite of a twinge of irritation at the way in which he included her in his answer, Sue couldn't suppress a small smile as she watched him attack his bacon and eggs with renewed zest. The anticipated pleasure of an evening out had cheered him. He might not realize it yet, but the pace of life at Glenroden was, for him, too slow. In time the quietness would only bore him. Unlike herself he was more suited to life in a big, bustling city.

On the evening of the outing Carlotte arrived late, and it was after six before they started out for Pitlochry. The autumn light was beginning to fade, but even so Sue enjoyed the change of scenery. She was surprised to find how quickly they arrived at the famous resort which lay in the beautifully wooded valley of the Tummel. To the east, Meric pointed out the mountains, faint shadows through the gathering darkness, and in the middle of the town the famous Clunie dam, part of the hydro-electric scheme with its fish-pass and observation chambers.

'You must take Tim before he returns to London and show him around,' he said smoothly, as they continued on through the town. 'You'll find more of interest there than you did on your tour of Glenroden.'

So he knew? Dismayed, Sue stared at the back of his strong dark head. Neither Tim nor she had mentioned where they had been, nor had they seen anyone who might have told him. When she had returned the map John hadn't even asked if they had had a good day. With a faint tinge of colour to her cheeks she tried to imagine how Meric could have found out. Was there anything going on at Glenroden which he didn't eventually hear about?

Carlotte broke the uneasy silence with a laugh, but she only managed to make things worse by saying, 'Are you returning for Christmas, Mr. Mason? I'm sure you would have fun, and Susan is going to be very lonely when you go back.'

Whatever Tim might have replied was lost as Meric swung abruptly through a pair of tall, wrought iron gates, jerking the car to a sudden stop in front of a large, imposing-looking hotel. 'It stays open all the year round,' he told them, as if anticipating Sue's query. 'But during winter months they rely quite a bit on local trade.' He opened the car door and got out. 'Come on in,' he said.

Nothing loath, they allowed him to pilot them indoors. Carlotte and Sue went to leave their cloaks in the ladies' room before joining the two men in the cocktail bar. Again Sue thought how splendid Meric looked in the kilt. He had a breadth of shoulder and height which made every other man in the room insignificant. Beside him she didn't notice Tim at all.

As they were late they carried their drinks to the dining-room. Sue sipped hers as she gazed around. It was a beautiful room with a tartan carpet and long wide windows, which during the daytime and the long summer evenings must provide wonderful views of the Scottish countryside.

She sat beside Tim, but Meric sat on her right and all through the varied, well-cooked meal she was aware of him – aware of him, it seemed, with every part of her being. Time and again her eyes were drawn to his darkly handsome face as if held there against her will. She had worn her black skirt, still all she had with her, but with it this time a soft clinging top of matching silk jersey with long sleeves and a low, rounded neckline which showed the pure, graceful lines of her throat and shoulders. Her heavy fair hair she had brushed until it clouded around her shoulders, spilling across her cheeks, giving her an occasional line of retreat.

Meric thought she looked attractive. She could see it in the appreciative gleam in his eyes as they rested on her slim figure, but he didn't say so in so many words. Somehow she ached that he should. Tim had no such inhibitions, yet his openly expressed admiration proved no balm for her sore heart.

After dinner they went into the ballroom and had coffee at one of the small tables arranged around the dance floor. A piper came in dressed in full Highland costume, and an impromptu concert was followed by dancing to a small Highland band. Later Sue found herself circling the room in Meric's arms.

'It's good of you to condescend to dance with me, Miss Fraser,' he murmured. 'I wonder that you trust your toes to a clumsy chap like me?'

'Don't apologize, Mr. Findlay,' she smiled, in the same vein. 'If you tread on my toes I shall no doubt find some means of retaliation, you may be sure.'

'Don't you always?' he retorted suavely, glancing keenly down at her. 'Is Tim Mason your latest form of retaliation?'

'Tim?' Her feet stumbled and she almost fell against him. 'How could he be?'

'Well, he certainly doesn't exert himself to please me.' Meric's hold tightened with slight cruelty on her waist as he swung her around, and his voice grew cooler. 'I might last out over the week-end, but I couldn't guarantee my temper much longer than that.'

Sue flushed, whether with dismay or annoyance she couldn't say. Perhaps it was a mixture of both. 'He's due to leave on Monday or Tuesday,' she replied stiffly.

'Just so long as he doesn't extend his visit,' he said dryly. 'Or that you ask him back.'

'You've not exactly gone out of your way to make him welcome,' she said sharply, stung to open rebellion by his derisive tone. 'What about your famous Highland hospitality?'

'It isn't always extended without discrimination. Not everyone is greeted with open arms.'

'But you can't slay people with a claymore these days just because you don't like them!'

'True.' His eyes glinting beneath raised brows brought a flare of colour to her cheeks. 'Words are about the only weapons left to us, but we have been known, even in this day and age, to use something stronger.'

Sue shivered slightly as his eyes slewed over her. Was he referring to their deer-stalking trip to the mountains? The thought of that day tinged her next words with an unintended hint of desperation. 'I can't imagine Tim will want to come back, even if you were to ask him!'

'Don't worry, I won't.' The glint in his eyes hardened, confirming that he misconstrued her reaction. 'He's no good to you, Sue. He's not your type at all with his mealy-mouthed ways. And the sooner you forget about him the better.'

'Why, you . . .' Quickly furious, Sue tried to escape from his arms. She hadn't a great deal of enthusiasm for Tim herself. From the time he had first called on her mother, a pleasant young man from the Tax Office obligingly leaving some forms on his way home, he had become more of a habit. But, she assured herself, if nothing else, she owed him a little loyalty. 'If I wanted to ask him, or any of my friends, to Glenroden, you couldn't stop me,' she gasped.

'Just try me and see!' Meric's grin was wholly mocking as he pulled her closer, stilling her struggles as the lights faded low for the end of the waltz. She felt herself slump against him, completely without defences as his breath quickened in her ear. 'I should enjoy a fight with you, sweet Sue, and I know who would be the victor.'

When the lights went up again with the close of the waltz, she left him, retiring blindly to her seat, aware that he followed at a more leisurely pace. Tim she found deep in conversation with Carlotte, who had her hand on his arm, obviously giving him her whole attention. Uneasily Sue remembered thinking Carlotte would not be above questioning Tim if she got the opportunity, and she had little doubt what those questions would be about. Carlotte had been told little except that Sue's parents had been separated, but Sue imagined her curiosity knew no bounds.

'You don't seem to have enjoyed that very much.' Leaving Tim, Carlotte rose to her feet, a mocking lilt to her voice as her eyes went from Sue's flushed face to where Meric lingered a few yards behind, exchanging a word with another man. 'You seem to be running away.'

'I didn't run away.' Sue drew a deep breath, adding with daring indifference, 'You do like to give the wrong impression.'

'It was you who was giving it, not I, dashing down the room as if wild animals were chasing you.' Undisturbed, Carlotte countered, 'As a matter of fact I've been enjoying a cosy chat with Tim. He's been telling me a little of your previous history. You're on the make, he appears to think, by coming to Glenroden. I really must relate the gist of it to Meric.'

Bewildered, her mouth slightly open, Sue stared after her,

as she turned to join Meric for the next dance. She had been foolish to imagine she could ask Carlotte about a job when she was so patently her enemy!

The evening continued with Highland dances, mostly reels, until it was time to go home. Tim didn't dance, but Meric, to Sue's surprise, danced a lot, although he didn't ask her again. But they joined with another party, comprising several young people from the neighbourhood, so Sue suffered no lack of partners. Fortunately she had taken Highland dancing in evening class, as part of a keep-fit curriculum at college, and being particularly light on her feet was no mean performer. She took part eagerly, hoping her rather forced enthusiasm successfully hid the longing in her heart for a tall, handsome Highlander who never came near her.

The two girls were tired when they arrived back at Glenroden and went straight to their rooms. Carlotte was staying for the night as it was too late to return to Perth. Unhappily Sue wondered if Meric had deliberately arranged it this way. Yet if he had romance in mind he didn't seem inclined to linger with Carlotte in the still warm drawing room where Mrs. Lennox had left out sandwiches and coffee in a flask in case they were hungry. After a very short time he followed them upstairs to bed. Sue heard him walk past her bedroom door, then there was silence apart from the wind blowing down the glen.

The wind usually lulled her to sleep, but on this occasion, an hour later, she was still lying awake. Her thoughts disturbed her, refusing to allow her to rest. Wholly they concentrated on Meric, clinging to him feverishly, turning the whole problem of Glenroden over and over in her mind. She knew beyond doubt that she loved him, although she realized the hopelessness of such misplaced affection. If she had ever had cause to hope, those hopes had been more than dashed this evening when he had practically ignored her existence. Sue shivered and tilted her head back on her pillows, letting a cool stream of air from the window play over her face and neck as she pushed back her heavy hair from her hot forehead. Then, exhausted by tossing and turning, she lay still, trying to remember everything he had said during their one dance. Not that there was a deal of comfort to be gained from that! He had lectured her about Tim; on whom she might not invite to Glenroden. He had talked as if he had actually owned the place! Suddenly, as her thoughts turned back, Sue sat straight up in bed.

Frowning through the darkness, she recalled how, when they had toured the estate, Tim had suggested that she searched the office to try and discover Meric's true position. Of course she had refused to have anything to do with such a scheme, and he hadn't mentioned it since. Now, at this very moment, she found such an idea curiously tempting – not from Tim's completely mercenary point of view but rather regarding her own relationship with Meric. From a personal angle it would make no difference to her feelings whether he was manager or not, but there was a possibility that he really was her father's partner. Or, worse than that, he could probably own half or even more of Glenroden. The thought had never occurred to her before. She couldn't think why not, but suddenly it seemed imperative that she knew the truth.

As she thought this, her eyes flew open, and with a quick twist of her supple body she pushed back the blankets and slid out of bed. Not stopping to put on her dressing-gown or slide her feet into a pair of slippers, she made for the door and gently opened it. She dared not switch on a light, and if she were to fumble after these things, someone might hear.

She need not have worried. The big house was silent, but she felt the palms of her hands go moist and sticky as she waited to make sure there wasn't anyone around. Reassured by the quietness, she slipped through the door, closing it carefully behind her before running down the thickly carpeted stairs to the hall, her bare feet making no sound.

The library which Meric used as an office lay along a passage at the back of the stairway. Wraith-like, Sue moved towards it with only memory and instinct to guide her. Otherwise there was only a very faint gleam of light from the moon coming in through an uncurtained glass pane high up on the wall. The only noise she could hear was her own heart beating too loudly in her ears.

At the library door she stopped, of a sudden drawn back within herself in an agony of uncertainty. Then resolutely, feeling that her decision had been a right one, she thrust open the door and went in. Once inside she stumbled, then paused on the threshold, wishing she had remembered to bring a torch. There was one in the kitchen, but somehow she didn't dare risk returning for it. The kitchen was full of bits and pieces, she might easily knock something over. As her fingers nervously flicked down the switch she waited apprehensively, but no one was likely to see a light at this time of night, and the sooner she found what she was looking for the better.

A quiver ran through her as she stared around the room. She had only been here once or twice before, once when she had come to collect Meric's dog for a walk – Carlotte had been here then – and another occasion with a message from a caller. She remembered the desk, but little more. Now her gaze wandered tentatively to the high bookshelves, the comfortable chairs by the wide fireplace before coming back to rest on the large oak desk with its leather-covered top. Then, suddenly, her heart was beating so heavy and fast it was unbearable, and her eyes widened with perplexity. It was a frightful thing, but now that she was here she found she couldn't go through with it. It had been an idea, impulsively born in a moment of stress, but Sue knew, standing there, that whatever secrets the old desk contained it must keep them. To start and search, even though it was her father's property, was something quite foreign to her nature, if only she had had the sense to realize this before. Perhaps, she thought despairingly, if after Tim was gone she came here and asked Meric frankly, he would tell her all she wanted to know.

CHAPTER TEN

In a moment of enlightenment which should have brought only relief, Sue suddenly found herself freezing into immobility. Instinctively she knew that someone stood outside the door. And when the door opened slowly, although it scarcely made any noise, the faint creak of the turning knob rang like an explosion in her ears.

After one suspended, crystalline moment she spun, like a top out of control, stunned disbelief illuminating her features as her shattered glance fell on Meric. Taut with despair, she stared at him, wondering speechlessly if he intended to strangle her. Every vestige of colour left her face as she heard him mutter some violent exclamation beneath his breath. As if the sight of her standing beside his desk aroused feelings of unrestrained anger.

For the first time since she had known him, his fury appeared to leave him incapable of words, and, because she couldn't seem to stand it any longer, she managed to speak.

'I'm sorry,' she stammered stupidly, through the heavy frightened beating of her heart. 'I didn't mean to disturb anyone. I don't know how you came to know I was here.'

His dark eyes narrowed even further as his cold, glittering glance went over her; the thick fall of hair, bare feet; the thin blue cotton boy's pyjamas. 'I came down to see if John was all right,' he said grimly. 'I followed you downstairs. It was dark and like you I didn't put on a light, but I didn't know who the cat-burglar was until I opened this door. I thought perhaps it was your friend Mr. Mason, taking a look around.'

'Is Father ill?' Fear took her breath, stinging through her head, so that she scarcely heard the last bit about Tim.

He replied harshly, 'You're changing the subject, Sue. He hasn't been well lately. You know that.'

Remorse caught her, but with it a flicker of indignation which seemed to dispel a fraction of fear. She met his eyes. 'I should have looked in myself when we came home, but I did think he'd be sleeping. And I'm not changing the subject!'

'No?'

It was just one word, but seemed to speak volumes. Her eyes clung to his, widening apprehensively. In his dressing gown he looked larger than usual, the breadth of his shoulders solid beneath the dark blue silk. He seemed older, entirely unapproachable, his hard face completely devoid of sympathy. He took a step nearer, continuing to watch her. The room was intensely quiet, and she wondered if he could hear the frantic thudding of her heart.

'You haven't told me what you were doing in my desk?' he rapped out, with such force she winced.

'I wasn't in your desk.' Stiffening with resentment, she tried to conjure up some gesture of defiance as she tilted her chin. From this angle she could see the terse set of his jaw, the dark, downy hair on his chest where his pyjamas lay open at his throat. Her resolution wavered as, with a quickly indrawn breath, she dragged her eyes away. She was aware that he waited, that if he was to believe her she must think of something convincing to add to her brief statement. But for a second time her mind refused to function and she remained silent – an uncertain, self-condemnatory silence.

Meric's dark eyes scanned her face. He insisted without mercy, 'If you weren't here to go through my desk, then what exactly were you doing? You'd better have a good explanation!'

Once before, Sue remembered, he had accused her of being a liar. It had only been said in jest, but she didn't want him to have an occasion to accuse her seriously. Yet what could she say? Despairingly she stepped backwards, away from that unnerving gaze. How was she to get out of this one when she hadn't the courage to admit the truth?

He gave her no longer than ten seconds before his patience broke. With one stride he reached her, his hands clamping down on her shoulders, gripping tightly through the thin cotton. 'Mason put you up to this, didn't he? You're trying to cover up!'

His question, like his hands, hurt. Hurt because in a way, he was right. Yet how could she possibly explain that her involvement was completely divorced from Tim's suggestion! It was impossible to involve Tim when she hadn't intended to share with him anything she might discover. And if she did confess any of this to Meric he would never believe she had changed her mind at the last moment. It was all too irrational to ring true.

Helplessly she shook her head, attempting to squirm from his hold. 'Tim doesn't know I'm here tonight in your office. That I swear.'

'Which doesn't really answer my question, as well you know!' Disregarding her feeble struggles, his fingers bit deeper as his temper increased.

Sue found herself stammering wildly, 'I know it was silly of me to come here. Perhaps I was sleepwalking, but I've done no harm. I haven't even touched your desk, and I certainly haven't stolen anything, in spite of what you suspect!'

If her tone of voice was meant to annihilate then she failed dismally as his mouth twisted sarcastically. 'You're wasting your time. You certainly weren't sleepwalking, although you might have been, dressed as you are!' His eyes, once more, went narrowly over her thin attire in such a way as to bring a deep flush to her white cheeks. 'I must admit,' he went on, 'that those pyjamas are better than what you were wearing in London, but even these don't leave much to the imagination. Maybe because they're too small.'

'I hate you!' Pent-up emotion released the words in a

rush as, stunned, she realized for the first time how very scanty were her pyjamas. Defensively she tried to wind her arms about her nerveless body.

He taunted, 'When a man finds a girl going through his property at this hour he's not usually bothered as to how she feels exactly.'

'You wouldn't have found me,' she cried witlessly, 'if you hadn't been sneaking around yourself. You gave me a horrible shock, creeping up behind me, and then you accuse me of all sorts of things . . .'

'Sue!' He interrupted the hysterical flow, shaking her none too gently. 'Are you going to tell me, or do I have to drag it out of you?'

His face was now as pale as her own, and his dark eyes cold, but keyed up, nerves jangling, she ignored the danger signals. Lips tightly closed, she made no response, just stared at him mutinously.

'So . . .' he ground out, his voice hard with anger, 'you enjoy being insolent! I've told you once in the past few hours and I'm telling you again. I don't have to spell it out. Get rid of Tim Mason, or heaven help me, I'll do it for you – which could be a lot more humiliating for him!'

Sue gasped on a wave of pure apprehension. 'Don't you dare say anything to Tim, do you hear me! Or he won't be the one to go, I can tell you.'

'Could that be a threat, Miss Frazer?' His fingers tightened ominously on her shoulders before sliding to grip the soft flesh of her arms, imbuing swift terror.

How could she answer him? How could she say – 'I have to find out your exact position at Glenroden? Not knowing is driving me crazy' – But there was her father to be considered. Suddenly, as confession trembled impulsively on her lips, this angle struck her. It was John who must tell her what she wanted to know, not this grim-faced man who held her so hurtfully because she refused to give him the explanation he asked for. She must have been blind not to have seen this before!

Little beads of perspiration appeared on her upper lip as her bewildered mind veered back to Tim. At all costs she must save him from Meric's anger. 'I don't like to see people hurt,' she faltered, 'especially Tim.'

He treated her short statement to the contempt he obviously thought it deserved. 'You seem determined to protect Mr. Mason,' his voice slurred sarcastically, 'so why isn't he around to protect you now from the scoundrel who runs Glenroden? Is he sitting up in bed, I wonder, waiting for whatever it was you intended to bring him?'

'You're quite, quite horrible!' Her face scarlet with temper, Sue felt she was stifling beneath the force of her indignation.

His hands left her so suddenly she almost fell. He spoke with soft violence. 'So – in your estimation I'm quite without virtue?'

'You could say that!' she retorted recklessly, her only desire to hurt with primitive intensity as she backed away from him. She swallowed something hard in her throat, moved again as the expression in his eyes changed darkly. She felt herself beginning to shake and knew that for the rest of her life she would remember this moment. There was a peculiar tenseness in the air between them, then no air at all, just an inexorable sensation of disaster as Meric advanced, his arms reaching out, this time not asking for explanations.

He came straight on, not stopping, taking hold of her, hauling her to him, ignoring her brief, futile struggles with a hard laugh. 'You must allow the devil to live up to his name,' he demanded, as with unleashed savageness he pulled her softly sensitive body into his arms.

Desperately she tried to fight, to escape, but he scornfully stilled her protests with brute strength, one hand hard on her throat, forcing her chin upwards, his lips hurting as they crushed heavily down on her own. Wildly the blood seemed to thunder through her veins, coursing like fire. It wasn't exactly like the time in the cottage, or on the mountain. He wasn't playing with her now, but neither was he loving her as his lips held her quivering mouth with a cruelty she had had no idea he possessed. Flame leapt through her body as weakly she tried to resist him, to hang on to one last shred of saneness. But her ineffectual movements he curbed with the strength of his arms, caressing her slight body until she slumped helplessly against the hard muscles of his chest.

Sensitively, driven by a surge of feeling, her arms lifted, locking behind his neck, her fingers moving unconsciously across his face, losing herself entirely in the violence of emotion which swept through her.

Only once did he lift his head, and only so his hand could explore the soft curve of her shoulder, linger on the bare, soft skin before sweeping the warm, silken hair back from her neck and burying his lips in the white pulsing hollow of her throat. His hands held her, allowing no protest, inflicting punishment, taking a cruel revenge for her rebelliousness. But, inadvertently, as his lips returned to hers, his love-making aroused a response which she had never known was possible, a shattering sensation of nerves and impulses, dissolving any self-control she might have left. Deliberately, it seemed, he set out to demonstrate how ineffectual was her resistance, what he could do to her if he wished. So that, when he stopped kissing her, her arms pulled his mouth down to hers again, uncaring whether he thought her wanton or not.

She had no idea how long afterwards she was aware that he lifted her in his arms and walked out of the office, back up the stairs in the moonlight, her soft, fluid body held close against him, her hair floating cloud-like through the cool, scented darkness. As he thrust open the bedroom door she heard him murmur inaudibly against her cheek, his lips soft on her hot skin, his tone speaking of a fast dwindling restraint. Then, so suddenly that the shock of his rejection shattered, he dropped her unmercifully back on to her bed,

His voice, as it came to her dazed bereft ears, was coolly sardonic, full of total mockery as he moved away. 'There comes a time, Sue, when the truth has to be forced upon us. A girl like yourself who's too blind to see otherwise . . .'

There came a sharp click of the door and he was gone, leaving her bruised body and mind to try, with hopeless incompetence, to grasp the implications of what he had said.

The next day being Sunday, Meric took Carlotte back to Perth after lunch and didn't return until late evening. On Monday Tim departed for London, and on the Tuesday afternoon John Frazer died. He died quietly in his sleep while having his afternoon rest. In spite of the fact that it wasn't unexpected, Sue was stunned by the suddenness of his going, when Mrs. Lennox broke the news.

Sue had been out walking, exercising the dogs, trying to rid herself of a measure of heartache. She hadn't seen Meric all day, nor, she assured herself, did she want to. Not until her mind came to terms with her problem and found a solution. Failing this, she knew she couldn't remain any longer at Glenroden. If she hadn't been aware of this before, she knew it now, definitely. To stay could mean utter humiliation. After what had happened in the office she couldn't trust herself where Meric was concerned. How could she place herself in a position where her precarious self-control might slip any time when he disliked her so strongly?

Before going to Perth, to the station with Tim to see him off, Carlotte rang. 'It's about this temporary job, darling.' Her voice had been warm and friendly, as if they'd parted on the best of terms. 'I believe,' she continued, 'it's yours if you want it. You would have to see the Head, of course, and if you're really keen, it might lead to better things.'

Sue had called at the school and been accepted – just, she believed, because of availability. With one or two minor details to be complied with, she could start the following week. She could either stay in digs and return to Glenroden each week-end or, if John was not agreeable, she would travel in each day. Either way it would give her the breathing space she so desperately needed.

But before she could find an opportunity to even tentatively broach the subject, her father wasn't there any more to confide in. Sue could scarcely believe shock could affect her so greatly. Perhaps it was the culmination of several things, but she seemed to feel much worse this time than when she had lost her mother. Meric and Mrs. Lennox took everything off her hands, seeming to understand her grief without explanation. Carlotte sent a brief note of condolence, but didn't appear at all.

'She doesn't care for this sort of thing,' Mrs. Lennox explained dryly. 'No doubt she'll turn up for the funeral!'

Meric was friendly but completely detached, dealing with everything with sober competence. Always he seemed there to see callers and answer the telephone, unobtrusively in the background, yet proving a veritable tower of strength, his own sense of loss only apparent in the faint lines of strain about his firm mouth, the sombre darkness in the direct gaze of his eyes.

The next few days, Sue found, passed in a sort of daze. If ever she thought of the future it was only with her teaching post in view. About Glenroden she didn't think at all. It seemed the natural sequence of things that the estate should go to Meric, although how this should be dealt with she had no idea. To her surprise she could muster up no interest.

But the day after the funeral she decided to go to Perth, to see John's solicitor and ask his advice. It had been arranged that he should come to Glenroden the following Monday, but on Monday, Sue knew, she wouldn't be here. Guiltily she realized Meric should have known this. In fact she had been going to tell him, but hadn't got round to it. During the week-end she must find the courage to approach him, but before this it seemed imperative that she saw this solicitor in Perth.

She left on Friday after an early lunch, having managed to get an appointment for two o'clock. To her relief Meric was out. In spite of the difference her journey to Perth seemed strangely reminiscent of that day in summer when she had seen her mother's solicitor about the letter which had brought her all the way north to Scotland in the first place. She remembered she had lunched beforehand with Tim. Erratically her thoughts roved as she drove swiftly towards the city. Maybe she ought to have let Tim know about her father? It would have been polite, only she had forgotten all about him since he had returned to London. He had simply faded from her mind since she had seen him off at the station. He didn't seem real any more. Only Meric Findlay occupied her heart and thoughts, but, after the un- happiness of losing John, not even Meric could dissolve the encompassing numbness.

Parking the car, she wandered along Marshall Place, to find the solicitor eventually some way further on, in a very ancient-looking building of no architectural distinction but which was probably known as a rare relic because of its obvious age. It was hemmed in by warehouses, public houses, and factories, with nothing to recommend it to the eye, but Sue was so relieved to find it she didn't notice these things. Inside, the dim interior managed to give an air of surprising comfort even though it was a trifle austere, but there was nothing comforting in what the solicitor had to say.

'You know, of course,' he began, 'that your father didn't own Glenroden? Not since he sold it ten years ago. He was indeed fortunate in finding a buyer like Meric Findlay. But there, that's water under the bridge, long since past.'

Aghast, Sue stared at him, unduly grateful that in his concentration with some papers he hadn't seemed to notice her start of surprise. So Meric owned Glenroden, not her father! And this man took it for granted she had known. Despair surged as she wondered desperately why John hadn't told her. Why he had kept such a thing from her. And, without the humiliation of confessing she knew nothing, how was she to acquire all the facts? She didn't even feel able to ask why her father had been forced to sell in the first place, as the solicitor would expect her to know this, too.

The man talked on. It was apparent he had known her father for years, her mother, too, after John married, although, true to his calling, he was studiously discreet.

'You're very like your grandmother, my dear. She was a fine woman,' he observed shrewdly, some time later as he personally saw Sue out.

When the door closed gently behind her, Sue realized that, apart from the one devastating piece of news, she was not much wiser than when she had come in. There had been something, she couldn't seem to remember the exact details, about a small legacy, but that was all.

Afterwards she had no clear recollection as to how she spent the remainder of the afternoon. For a while she just wandered. In a small café she ordered tea, but could not remember eating it, nor leaving after she had paid the bill. It had long been dark before she found her way back to Glenroden, and it was only as she crossed the ford that she decided to say nothing to Meric of what she knew until she left again on Monday morning. Then it would necessarily have to be brief. A short apology – a word of farewell and thanks before a quick departure. It would all be over in a few minutes, saving a lot of embarrassment. Meric would probably be grateful. Explanations, should he choose to ask or give any, would be almost impossible because of time. At all costs, Sue argued with herself, she must keep everything down to a bare minimum, otherwise, in her present highly emotional state, she might say things which she would later regret.

This evening Meric would be out when she returned. Thankfully she recalled that he had an appointment which he had said couldn't be put off. Deliberately she had tarried in Perth until she knew he would be gone, not realizing she was getting cold. As she walked aimlessly around the streets, the air had been chill, and she hadn't remembered that the heater in the car had developed a fault during summer which hadn't been put right. Now she was indeed frozen, and longed suddenly for a hot cup of tea.

Her headlights swept the short drive brightly as she drove up to the front of the house, and she switched them off swiftly so that she might no longer see the old stone façade of a house which could be home to her no more. Quickly she jumped out on to the gravel, leaving the car where it was, and ran with stumbling feet in through the main front entrance.

With numbed fingers she caught and slammed the door behind her, only then becoming aware that, in spite of all her precautions, Meric was there, striding down the hall towards her, his shabby old working kilt swinging, his hard face grim. He was almost on top of her before she could think of a means of escape.

'Sue!' His terse exclamation jolted her to a stop as his glance took in her white face, the wide, shadowed eyes, the nervous tremor which ran through her slight figure, oddly attired in a thin summer coat. 'Sue, for God's sake, where have you been!' Impatiently he grabbed her shoulders and shook her, the force of his emotions transferring through his hands, so that all her newly made resolutions crumpled and tears started streaming in torrents down her cheeks.

'Sue!' For the third time he uttered her name, but this time his voice held more than a hint of desperation. 'Please tell me what's wrong, what's happened?'

When she made no reply because she couldn't, he caught her shaking body to him, one hand behind her head, holding her against his shoulder, cradling her in his arms until the force of her pent-up misery exhausted itself. And all the time he kept repeating, 'Sue darling, I love you.'

From somewhere, it seemed a great distance, eventually she heard, yet was unable to take in the full implication of what he was saying. Stupidly her mind clung to what she had learnt that afternoon, as helplessly she tried to free her hand, to scrub away her tears with a clenched fist.

'Why didn't you tell me?' she whispered brokenly.

His body went instantly rigid against her own, and the hand which had been stroking her hair stopped suddenly as he withdrew fractionally. He went on holding her, but his eyes were inscrutable, his mouth tightening grimly as he realized her question was quite divorced from what he had been murmuring. 'Just where the devil have you been this afternoon?' he insisted curtly.

This time there was no possible evasion, yet she hesitated, guilt that she hadn't trusted Meric sweeping through her, mingling with despair. 'You didn't guess?' she whispered, her breath catching in her throat.

'Sue, how could I?' His eyes lingered with attempted patience, a growing anxiety, on her tear-wet cheeks. 'Mrs. Lennox thought you'd gone to Perth, but when you didn't come back I began to worry. I've been nearly out of my mind!'

'You were going out to dinner.' There was still a sob in her voice which she couldn't control.

'It wasn't important.' He dismissed his engagement with a terse shrug of his shoulders. 'You are! I took Mrs. Lennox to the village, expecting to find you home when I returned. But that doesn't answer my question.'

There could be no escape. Apprehensively she forced her head up to meet his eyes. 'I went to see Father's solicitor in Perth,' she said.

'Ferguson?'

She nodded mutely, feeling faintness. What had she done? Meric's face swayed strangely. She cried out as his grip tightened, but before she could speak he picked her up, and, with the dampness of her cheek against his jacket, strode with her to the library. With a resounding thud he closed the door.

Through a haze Sue sank willingly into the strength of his arms, conscious that here was great joy. Yet also she was aware of a growing consternation when she thought of all which must be said, all of which she had hoped to avoid. Vaguely, as Meric held her, sat down with her on the great leather settee, she recalled some whispered words of endearment. He might only have intended bringing comfort? Whatever – he certainly wouldn't care for her any more when he learned how she had gone behind his back!

Nervously weak, she forced herself to speak. 'I was only trying to find out about the estate. I had a horrible feeling that things were not as they should be. Sometimes I thought you were only a domineering manager, but, at others, I had a frightening conviction that Father and I were living on charity.'

'Poor Sue – so mixed up . . .' Above her head his warm voice deepened to tenderness. 'Suppose,' he suggested firmly, 'we start at the beginning, you and I? Something we should have done long ago.'

She looked up, meeting the stern concern in his eyes, and felt the grip of his hands tighten. 'This solicitor, he told me you own Glenroden, not Father, but I didn't ask him anything else. He seemed to take it for granted I should know. I could scarcely tell him I knew nothing. Besides, it didn't seem important any more.'

His eyes held hers, not condemning but full of regret as he regarded her pinched, colourless face. 'If only I'd known where you were going, Sue! I could have saved you all this heartache. I intended explaining everything over the weekend. I was only giving you a breathing space which I thought you needed. I was definitely going to tell you before Ferguson came on Monday.'

'I see,' she said, but she didn't, and waited silently for him to go on. He still held her and her heart fluttered in her throat, threatening to choke her. She dared not move for fear he left her and, if nothing else, she must have this moment to hold for ever.

'When I bought Glenroden ten years ago,' he told her, 'I was a callow youth of twenty-five who didn't know the first thing about farming in the Highlands. Glenroden was on the market and I bought it.'

'Just like that!'

'Just like that, sweet Sue. Haven't you discovered that when I see something I want I must have it?' Her pulse jerked again as he punished her small interruption. He went on, 'The estate wasn't entailed and John's brother – your uncle, I suppose – had sold off most of the farms. From what I gather he lived very much beyond his means. There had only been Glenroden left, and this was heavily mortgaged. John fought against losing odds for years. He had no family – he didn't then know about you. But having to part with Glenroden hurt him a lot.'

Sue flinched, asking as he paused, 'You let him stay?'

His mouth quirked ruefully. 'Not then from any feeling of benevolence, I'm afraid. To me it made sense. John knew everything there was to know about the running of a Highland estate. I had no knowledge whatsoever. We came to an arrangement.'

'You mean . . . he was the manager?'

Meric shook his head. 'No, Sue, not that. I liked to manage my own affairs, even then. But he taught me all I had to know and lived with me here at Glenroden. In fact, very few people knew the true position.'

'But surely, when you bought it . . .'

'It suited me, Sue, for reasons of my own. Remember I once told you my father died in South Africa? Well, my mother married again and I didn't exactly see eye to eye with my stepfather. At twenty-five one is young enough and often crazy enough for anything. I took my share, pulled out and came here. But I didn't want my family following on my heels, which, if they'd known about Glenroden, they might have done. My mother is Scottish born too, you see.'

'And the family now?'

'Oh, nice and tight in S.A. It was the step I was seeing in London when I took you down. He wanted to see me about some shares I still have in the mine.'

'So that was what you were doing?'

'What else?' His eyebrow tilted.

Sue stared hard at a leather button on his jacket. 'I thought perhaps you were with Carlotte . . .'

'And I thought you were painting the town red with Mr. Mason! It seems we both jumped to the wrong conclusions, my darling.'

There was silence, a long-drawn-out moment when Meric's arms drew her closer, while Sue tried to take in what he'd just told her. There were still several things she didn't understand. 'Why didn't Father tell me about it,' she whispered at last, 'when I first came?'

His eyes met hers soberly. 'We should have told you, but John begged me not to. I think subconsciously he was frightened of losing you, as he did your mother, and he imagined, rightly or wrongly, that if he told you the truth you might go. He did intend doing so after a while, but like most deceptions the knot became increasingly difficult to unravel. And, on top of this, his health didn't improve, which made it daily more difficult for me to insist on a course of positive action.'

In spite of the warmth from the fire and Meric's arms, Sue felt suddenly cold. 'Why didn't he trust me?' she said sadly. 'I was his daughter, I should never have left him. That is—' Her face whitened as she remembered her new job. How was she to explain this? Yet somehow it was easier than she'd thought. Everything seemed easier now with

185

Meric. 'I only intended staying away during the week,' she finished, 'or even going in daily; whatever he wanted. I just felt I ought to be earning my keep.' No need, she decided hollowly, to mention to Meric that it had really been a means of escape from him.

But Meric glanced at her keenly, almost as if he guessed the truth. 'Your father would have told you eventually, Sue. Perhaps on the whole life had proved too disillusionary for him to trust people too easily. In many ways he certainly seemed happier after you came, but, as things turned out, he wasn't given the time to prove it.'

'As you say,' Sue mused sadly, 'maybe neither of us was given enough time, but I didn't realize until after he'd gone that I was beginning to love him dearly. It is some comfort to know I helped a little. But,' she added dully, 'he must have trusted you implicitly.'

'I think he did.' Meric paused, regarding her thoughtfully. 'Ten years, Sue, is a long time. We got on very well together, he and I. I think he regarded me as he might have done his own son if he'd had one. Certainly I grew fond of him. It's been heartbreaking this last year to see his good health diminish so rapidly.'

He regarded her a moment longer, then in the ensuing silence slid her gently from his knees on to the settee, proceeding with deft fingers to remove her coat. As she shivered slightly he jerked it from her shoulders, examining the thinness of it sombrely. 'You needed money, I expect, to replace this sort of thing? I told John to ensure you had enough, but he obviously never got round to it.'

Sue shook her head, evading a direct reply, startling herself by answering his question with a totally impulsive one of her own. 'You never wanted to get married?'

'Yes,' he replied softly, 'many times.'

So it was Carlotte! Apprehensively Sue stared at him, her eyes wide, dilating, the newly restored colour fading from her cheeks. The dizziness returned, and she was scarcely aware that he was back beside her on the settee until he placed a glass between her shaking fingers, commanding her to drink it. 'I should have given you that when you first came in,' he frowned, 'but I was too distracted to think straight. Drink it up, there's a good girl,' he ordered with mock sternness, 'then take a look at what I'm going to show you.'

As she sipped the brandy nervously, Sue's colour returned, but her eyes still stayed on him fearfully.

From his pocket he took his wallet, and from it a small miniature, gazing at it for a moment like a star-struck teenager. Then he put it in front of her on a small table. It was a small oval miniature of a girl, a young girl in a flowered dress. Her fair hair was looped back into ringlets, and tiny feathery tendrils of hair escaped at her temples.

Bewildered, Sue stared. The girl in the miniature was an exact replica of herself, only it couldn't be! The high neck of the dress and the hair-style spoke of another age. Yet the likeness was amazing. 'Who is she?' she gasped. 'Where did you get it from?'

'I found it,' he exclaimed, with great satisfaction, 'by accident – in one of the bottom drawers of this desk. I did ask John if I could keep it, and he agreed. I knew then that she was the only girl I could marry, which was crazy, as I could never hope to meet her. Or so I thought – until one evening in Edinburgh . . .'

His meaning couldn't have been clearer. Sue's heart missed a great beat as her gaze left the other girl in the miniature to cling to Meric's face. 'You thought it was me?'

His hand clamped possessively over hers. 'I knew it was you,' he stated positively. 'Or, if you like, your grandmother reincarnated. That evening you obviously thought my behaviour peculiar.' He gave a slight smile. 'I suppose it was, but when a man sees a dream coming true he doesn't usually stop to think. Even when you took fright – very properly, I might say, and ran away – I knew beyond doubt you would turn up at Glenroden.'

'And you waited on the crag,' she whispered. 'And yet you were annoyed about something?'

'I waited on the crag,' he repeated, his arms going around her. 'And to begin with I was suddenly alarmed that you might upset John – thus the bad temper. I was annoyed more with myself than you, for not thinking of it sooner. Then you weren't a bit like the meek Victorian Miss of my dreams. You've been quite a little handful! Sometimes I wanted to shake you, especially when your Mr. Mason appeared, but,' he added wryly, 'in spite of all the misunderstandings I could never resist an opportunity to have you in my arms.'

'Darling,' Sue snuggled against him, warmly content. 'You don't need to worry about Tim. I never loved him, nor did I ever let him think I did. I think he was confused by many things, but I don't suppose he'll ever come back to Glenroden.' She finished helplessly, 'I've loved you for so long.'

'Not as long as I've loved you, Sue,' He kissed her deeply, tenderly. Then, on a lighter note, 'I'll admit when I first heard about Tim Mason, I thought you couldn't make up your mind.'

'I thought exactly the same about Carlotte Craig,' she retorted, but not quite so lightly.

He ran his fingers through her hair, brushing it back from her smooth forehead. 'What we have, Sue, is something stronger than lesser passions.' His deep voice vibrated. 'Do your teaching stint, darling, if you must, but marry me before Christmas. I refuse to wait any longer.'

'We'll spend Christmas at Glenroden?' she pleaded, hiding her hot face against his rough jacket. Everything seemed to be happening so quickly, she could scarcely take it in, but the knowledge that Meric Findlay loved her sent the blood singing wildly through her veins.

'Yes,' he agreed slowly, his dark eyes faintly smiling. 'We'll spend Christmas here at Glenroden, then I'll take you to South Africa for a proper honeymoon, and to meet the family. You'd like that?'

Sue nodded. Just so long as Meric was there she didn't mind where they went. They would come back to this old grey house amongst the mountains. From now on Glenroden would always be home – Father would like that ... In her heart she knew a warm prayer of thankfulness as Meric, as if understanding her thoughts, held her close.

Each month from Harlequin

8 NEW FULL LENGTH ROMANCE NOVELS

Listed below are the last three months' releases:

75c each

These titles are available at your local bookseller, or through the Harlequin Reader Service, M.P.O. Box 707, Niagara Falls, N.Y. 14302; Canadian address 649 Ontario St., Stratford, Ont. N5A 6W4.

Have You Missed Any of These
Harlequin Romances?

Have You Missed Any of These
Harlequin Romances?